ANGLO-SAXON
BOY

TONY BRADMAN has been writing children's books for over thirty years. He has written poetry and picture books, and lots of stories, including the highly successful Dilly the Dinosaur series, and was also lead author of the popular Project X primary reading scheme. In recent years he has turned more to historical fiction, and has written books set in a wide range of periods, from Roman Britain to the First and Second World War. Tony is also a reviewer of children's books, and has been a judge for the Smarties Book Prize, the Guardian Children's Fiction Prize and the BookTrust Teen Awards, and chairs The Siobhan Dowd Trust, a charity founded in memory of the writer Siobhan Dowd, which supports projects to bring the joy of reading to children from disadvantaged backgrounds. *Anglo-Saxon Boy* is Tony's second historical novel for Walker, a companion title to *Viking Boy*.

About *Anglo-Saxon Boy*, he says: "I was always fascinated by the story of Harold, the king who died at the Battle of Hastings in 1066, the last Anglo-Saxon monarch of England. When I was doing some reading about the period, I discovered that his son Magnus would have been about fifteen at the time of the battle – and suddenly I *had* to tell the story of Magnus and his father. And that's the story in this book."

Also by Tony Bradman:

Viking Boy

ANGLO-SAXON BOY

TONY BRADMAN

Illustrated by Sam Hart

WALKER BOOKS

First published in Great Britain 2017 by Walker Books Ltd
87 Vauxhall Walk, London SE11 5HJ

2 4 6 8 10 9 7 5 3 1

Text © 2017 Tony Bradman
Illustrations © 2017 Sam Hart

The right of Tony Bradman and Sam Hart to be identified as author and illustrator respectively of this work has been asserted by them in accordance with the Copyright, Designs and Patents Act 1988

This book has been typeset in Stempel Garamond LT Std

Printed and bound in Great Britain by Clays Ltd, St Ives plc

British Library Cataloguing in Publication Data:
a catalogue record for this book is
available from the British Library

ISBN 978-1-4063-6377-7

www.walker.co.uk

**THIS IS DEDICATED TO
THE ONE I LOVE**

"Þagalt ok hugalt skyli þjóðans barn
ok vígdjarft vera…"
(The son of a ruler should be quiet and watchful,
and skilled in warcraft…)

– The Havamal, or Words of the High One,
ninth-century Old Norse

"Him be healfe stod hyse unweaxen,
Cniht on gecampe, se full caflice
braed of ðam beorne blodigne gar…"
(Beside him in the battle stood a boy not fully grown,
who bravely pulled the bloody spear from his wound…)

– The Battle of Maldon, tenth-century Old English

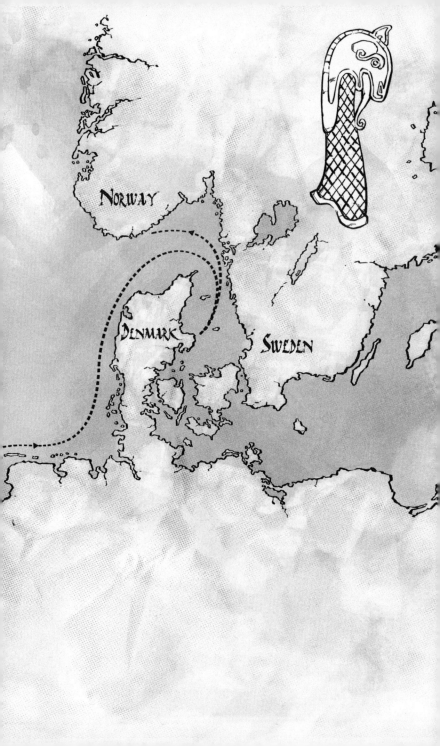

NORWAY

DENMARK

SWEDEN

CONTENTS

PROLOGUE
SENLAC RIDGE
14 OCTOBER 1066

*"Here they come again!"
somebody yelled, although
there was no need. Magnus
and everybody else in the
English shield-wall could see
the mass of men advancing
up the slope towards them,
the low autumn sunlight*

glinting off helmets and the blades of spears and axes. All along the top of the ridge the English tightened their grip on shield straps and weapons, stared ahead, waited for the shock of battle.

The dead lay between the two armies, and the grass was slick with blood beneath the boots of the living. Magnus felt the sweat running down his face from under his helmet, and the men on either side of him squeezing in more tightly, their chain-mailed arms grinding against his. He hefted his spear, pushed its shaft over the rim of his shield, rolled his shoulders to try and get the terrible aching out of them.

"Steady, lads!" another voice called out. Magnus craned round to look at the hill crest, where two banners streamed in the breeze, The White Dragon of Wessex and The Fighting Man. A knot of men was there too, chief among them his father. Their eyes met and his father nodded, but Magnus turned away – just in time to see the opposing shield-wall split, each half swiftly moving aside to leave a wide gap.

A squadron of mounted warriors with lances burst out of the gap and charged up the slope, the ground trembling beneath the hooves of the horses. Suddenly the sky darkened, and Magnus saw yet another cloud of arrows dropping towards the English line, the deadly barbed points slicing down through the air. The arrows arrived first, men screaming and falling, and then the horses crashed into them too.

The man to the left of Magnus died quickly, a lance ripping into his throat and out through the other side, flinging him backwards. The man beyond him stepped into his place, overlapping his shield with that of Magnus, both of them thrusting their spears up at the mounted warriors in front of them. One loomed over Magnus, chopping and hacking at him with a sword, trying to knock his shield down or smash it.

For a while the madness of battle took over, Magnus jabbing his spear at the horsemen, their wild-eyed, foam-flecked mounts rearing, lashing out with their iron-shod hooves. Blade clashed on blade, men yelled and cursed and grunted and fell dying around him, until at last he glimpsed a sword swinging in an arc, bright sunlight flashing like fire off its steel. He tried to duck, but wasn't quite fast enough.

15

There was a great CLANG! *as the sword hit his helmet, and he was knocked sideways, dropping his shield and falling across several bodies, hot blood running down the side of his face. The roar of battle faded and Magnus lay staring up at the cold blue sky, a bird circling far above. It looked like a kestrel, he thought, or perhaps a hawk, and it seemed to be moving further and further away...*

Darkness filled his mind like night falling.

ONE

DANGEROUS TIMES

FIFTEEN MONTHS EARLIER – MAY 1065

THE MESSENGER ARRIVED just as the sun was rising over the hills. Most people on the farm were

still asleep, but not Magnus – he had decided to go hunting in the woods that day. He was leaving the hall with a spear in his hand and a couple of hounds from the farm's pack at his heels when he heard someone calling from beyond the gates. The guard in the wooden watchtower looked down, then signalled to the two guards below, who raised the great bar across the gates and pulled them open.

A man rode into the courtyard on a chestnut stallion, and Magnus recognized him immediately. Hakon was a member of his father's bodyguard, the housecarls. The last time Magnus had seen him, Hakon had been in full war gear – in mail shirt and helmet, carrying shield and spear. But that had been on the war trail against the Welsh last autumn, and now Hakon wore ordinary clothes – red tunic, dun trousers, black cloak. His long fair hair was tied back, and his drooping moustache was neatly combed. All he had to mark him out as a warrior was the short sword hanging from his belt. That and his broad shoulders and the easy way he sat in the saddle.

"Is your mother awake, Magnus?" he said, jumping down from his horse. He spoke English well, but with an accent. Like many of the housecarls, Hakon was a Dane.

"I am wide awake," said a voice behind them. "Has something happened?"

Magnus turned and saw his mother framed by the carved posts of the hall doorway. She was wrapped in a simple blue gown, and the morning sun touched her hair with gold as if it were her due – people called her Edith the Fair. There was worry in her lovely face, though, and Magnus guessed why. They lived in dangerous times, and messengers often brought bad news.

"Not yet, my lady," said Hakon with a smile. "But it will soon. My lord the Earl Harold is nearly home. He sent me on ahead to tell you of his coming."

"I should have known he would play one of his tricks," she muttered, frowning. "I suppose he made you all ride through the night. How long do I have?"

Magnus smiled too. His father loved to take everyone by surprise. He was famous for it in war, often striking before his enemies had any idea he was even near.

"An hour at the most," said Hakon, grinning now.

"Well, don't just stand there, Magnus," his mother said. "We have work to do!"

She turned round and hurried back into the hall. Magnus heard her yelling at the servants and his brothers and sisters, and before long everyone was awake and dashing in different directions and colliding with each other. Magnus couldn't help thinking it was like watching a bee skep that had been knocked over, the bees buzzing around in sheer panic while their queen tried to render order out of chaos.

He knew his mother would do exactly that. She ran everything while his father was away, and she was very good at it. These days his father seemed to be away more often than not. It was mostly fighting, of course – against the Welsh, the Irish, Viking raiders. But Earl Harold Godwinson was a great man, a power in the land of the English, so he was often with the other great men at the court of King Edward.

"No hunting for you today then," said Hakon, leading his horse to the stables, a low building that formed one side of the courtyard and had room for fifty mounts.

Magnus shrugged and followed him. He was wary of Hakon. The housecarl was one of the best warriors in England, and he had looked after Magnus on the war trail, making sure his first campaign – at the age of fourteen – wasn't his last. Hakon had a sense of humour, but he was a hard man too, one who didn't suffer fools gladly.

The hounds, sensing they wouldn't be needed now, ran off across the courtyard. "I might try to slip out a bit later," said Magnus. "I doubt anyone will miss me."

"You couldn't be more wrong," said Hakon with a snort. "Your father told me to make sure I gave you a message as well, Magnus. He wants to talk to you."

"What about?" said Magnus, surprised. They had reached the stable doors and stood there for a moment. Magnus realized he had grown – last year Hakon had been a hand's breadth taller than him, and now his eyes were on a level with the housecarl's.

It was Hakon's turn to shrug. "He didn't say. You'll find out soon enough."

Hakon led the horse into the dark stables, leaving

Magnus alone with his thoughts. He wondered if he had done anything to anger his father since he had last seen him. Perhaps his father wasn't happy with how he had handled himself on the war trail. Earl Harold had fought a major campaign in North Wales two years ago, defeating and killing Gruffudd, Prince of Gwynedd, but last autumn he had only been chasing raiders. There hadn't been much real fighting – just a few skirmishes, an ambush or two – and Magnus hadn't made a single kill. He sighed, and headed for his favourite place to do some brooding, the orchard on the slope above the hall. He stuck his spear into the ground beside an apple tree and sat down, his back against the trunk.

Stretched out below him was the whole farm, although Magnus knew that was far too small a word to describe the family's rich holding. At its heart was the great hall with its long, whale-backed roof and crossed beams at both ends. Other buildings sur-rounded it – the stables, several large barns, animal sheds of one kind or another. A wooden palisade circled them all, a watchtower at the gate. Beyond were the wide paddocks with their herds of cattle and flocks of sheep, and further still were fields full of crops. It was late spring here on the coast of Sussex, the land of the South Saxons, and the wheat and barley was young and green in the furrows.

Southwards lay the village of Bosham that gave their manor its name. Magnus could see the square tower of the church above the thatched houses, the small harbour, the blue sea glittering in the low sunlight. This was where Godwin, his father's father, had begun the family's rise to power. Magnus had never met him – he had died before Magnus was born – but he had heard the stories. His grandfather had been an outsider with nothing, and he had fought and struggled and built until the Godwins were the greatest family in England, respected and feared by all.

Magnus knew most boys would give anything to be part of such a family, and of course he was proud to be a Godwin. But he was a very minor Godwin. His father was Earl of Wessex and owned vast swathes of land in Mercia and East Anglia. His father's sister – another Edith – was the king's wife, and therefore

23

Queen of England. His father's younger brothers, Tostig, Gyrth and Leofwine were earls as well. Magnus had two older brothers, both surely destined for great futures. How could he hope to match all that? He might just as well give up before he had even started.

When he went back, servants and slaves were still milling around inside the hall, but it had been swept and tidied, the fire lit in the great hearth, food and drink laid on the long tables – cold meat and cheeses and fresh loaves of bread, and great jugs of foaming ale and mead. His mother had changed into a dark green gown of the finest wool and had combed her long golden hair till it shone.

"Where have you been, Magnus?" she said. "I was beginning to think you'd run away. And why are you wearing those old clothes? You should change."

"These are fine, Mother," he said. "You're the one Father will be looking at."

"Oh Magnus, I wish that were true," she said, although he could tell she was pleased. "I'm sure he meets much more beautiful women all the time…"

"My lady, Earl Harold is at the gate!" cried a servant from the doorway.

She laughed and ran out of the hall. A crowd swept Magnus out after her – and there was his father riding into the courtyard at the head of his men, fifty housecarls on fine mounts. Earl Harold sat tall in the saddle of his great black stallion, his brown hair hanging to his shoulders, his moustache thicker and longer than Hakon's, his cloak blood-red. Magnus thought he looked magnificent, like a king. Behind the housecarls were the spare horses, each one carrying a warrior's weapons and armour, the round shields all bearing the same image, the White Dragon of Wessex.

Earl Harold jumped from his horse and strode up to the hall. "Now then, Edith, what have I done to make you frown at me like that?" he said, looking concerned. "I have ridden hard to get here, desperate as I am to see the fairest face in England."

Magnus glanced at his mother. "You know exactly what you've done, you rogue," she said, unable to stop herself smiling. "But I suppose I'll have to for-give you."

"That is all I could hope for, my lady," said Earl Harold, returning her smile, taking her hand so he could pull her close and kiss her. "Come, let us go into the hall and eat the feast I know you will have prepared for me. It is good to be home."

Magnus tried to catch his father's eye, but his parents swept past him and through the doorway, the crowd pushing and shoving each other as they followed.

It was nearly two more days till Magnus found out what his father wanted.

TWO

SURROUNDED BY ENEMIES

THERE WAS ALWAYS a buzz of pleasure about the place when the earl returned to his hall, especially if he had been away long. He was a ring-giver, a generous lord to his warriors, and a good provider to everyone else – nobody ever went hungry in the service of Harold Godwinson, not even the lowliest peasant or slave

27

in the years when the harvest was bad. But Magnus knew there was more to it than that. People served his father because they loved him, not because of what he gave them.

The earl was also their only source of justice. The people of the farm started lining up while he was still eating, begging him to listen to their complaints against others or settle disputes. Later in the morning people from Bosham and the neighbouring settlements started to arrive, and soon the hall was packed with a large, noisy crowd, all clamouring to be heard. Magnus found himself being elbowed out of the way again, and guessed his father would wait for a better moment to speak to him. But his mother had little patience with the crowd, and quickly lost her temper.

"Enough!" she yelled. "Hakon, clear these people out so the earl can rest!"

Hakon swiftly did as he was ordered, organizing the other housecarls to help him with the task. They pushed and shoved the crowd to the doorway and beyond, and before long the hall was more peaceful, just a few servants and the family remaining. Yet Magnus hung back, watching his brothers and sisters as they took their chance to chatter to their father, boasting about what they had been doing since he had seen them last, competing for his attention like a pack of over-excited puppies.

"I've been practising with the bow you gave me, Father," said Godwin. He was the firstborn, named for their grandfather, two years older than Magnus and the one who looked most like their mother. "Yesterday I hit the target ten times out of ten."

"Don't listen to him, Father, he's lying," said Edmund, the second child. He was a year older than Magnus, but dark and stocky – people said that showed the family must have Welsh blood some-where in its past. Godwin shoved him, and Edmund shoved back, but they soon stopped when their father gave them a look.

"Did you bring me the necklace, you promised, Father?" Gytha said sweetly. She was two years younger than Magnus and named after their grand-mother Gytha, who still lived. The younger Gytha was set to be a golden-haired beauty too.

"If Gytha gets a necklace, I want one as well!" said ten-year-old Gunhild, the youngest. She was the most mixed of them all, sometimes looking like their mother, sometimes their father, although like Magnus, her hair was copper-coloured.

"I'm sure there will be something for you in my saddlebags," said their father, laughing and squeezing Gunhild's cheek. "And what about you, Magnus?"

Magnus uneasily met his father's gaze, trying to think of an achievement he could boast about, and failing. He shrugged, and wondered if he should simply ask what his father wanted of him, but this didn't seem the right time or place. He didn't get the opportunity in any case, for just then Hakon returned to the hall.

"My lord, more people have come to speak to you," he said. "They won't take no for an answer, either. What do you want me to do with them?"

"Let them in," said the earl. "Duty calls, children. We'll talk more later."

* * *

He was kept busy for the rest of that day, and the next day turned out to be even worse. By late evening, Magnus had decided his father must have changed his mind about speaking to him, and tried not to think about it any more. But he couldn't sleep, and lay wide awake in the chamber he shared with his brothers, both of whom were snoring deeply. Suddenly Hakon appeared in the doorway and beckoned to him.

"Your father will see you now, Magnus," the housecarl said quietly.

Magnus rose and followed Hakon through the darkened hall. The fire in the central hearth had been allowed to die down for the night, and the floor beside the walls was lined with the humped shapes of sleeping servants and housecarls. Hakon and Magnus came at last to a large chamber at the rear of the hall, the place where the family documents and treasures were stored in chests. The chamber was lit by a dozen tall candles, the kind that always made Magnus think of church.

His father was sitting on a stool studying a scroll,

and looked up. "Thank you, Hakon," he said. The housecarl nodded and slipped away, back into the shadows of the hall. Somewhere in the night outside an owl hooted, and Magnus had a brief vision in his mind of the bird swooping down to seize a tiny mouse in its sharp talons. "Sit down, Magnus," said the earl. "Do you know what this document is?"

Magnus pulled up a stool and peered at the parchment, which was covered with lines and words. He had been taught to read by monks, as all noble children were. His brothers had always grumbled about it – they couldn't see the point, and were only interested in lessons that involved sword and spear and shield. But Magnus had enjoyed acquiring the skill, and he had seen other documents like this.

"It's a map, Father," he said. "It shows Britain and the lands nearby."

His father smiled. "Good. So you know this is England, the Kingdom of the Angles and Saxons – Wessex here in the south, Mercia and East Anglia across the middle, Northumbria beyond. We English rule most of Britain, but we're surrounded by enemies, and the day is coming when they might attack. King Edward will die soon, and the wolves are gathering. Many men think they should sit on his throne…"

Magnus had heard such things before. The monks who had taught him to read had taught him about the past too, so he knew that Britain had been fought over for hundreds of years. The Romans had taken it from the Welsh, built their great cities of stone, then left them to fall into ruins, and Britain to the Welsh once more. Then the Angles and Saxons had come from across the sea and founded their own kingdoms, penning the Welsh into the western mountains. There had been wars with the Scots in the far north, and the Irish had raided from their own island. The Angles and Saxons had fought amongst themselves, each kingdom struggling to rule the others.

After that the Vikings came, mostly from Denmark. They too began as raiders, but they seized land and started to settle, almost turning the east and north completely Danish – the Godwins were part Danish, grandmother Gytha being from a noble Danish family. King Alfred of Wessex defeated the Danes at last, and his grandson Athelstan united the Angles and Saxons – and even the Danes who had settled – into the Kingdom of England. But there were still raids, and wars big and small.

"Perhaps King Edward will live longer than everyone thinks, and have a son to succeed him," said Magnus. "That would make a difference, wouldn't it?"

His father frowned and shook his head. "It was your grandfather's dream for a Godwin to sit on the throne, one of his descendants. That's why he persuaded Edward to marry my sister – it seemed the easiest way. But they've been husband and wife for years and they've had no children."

"So who *will* succeed him then, Father? You must have some idea."

"It could be any one of half a dozen men with claims to the throne – or it could be me." The earl smiled. "Don't look so surprised, Magnus. I have plenty of supporters. Everyone knows England needs a strong ruler, now more than ever. And the truth is that Edward already depends on me to run his kingdom. But making a bid for the throne of England won't be easy – and I will need your help to make sure I don't fail."

Magnus realized his mouth was open, and he quickly shut it. His mind was reeling with surprise, yet the more he thought about it, the more it seemed to make sense. He was sure his father would make a magnificent King of England – nobody would be better. He was a great warrior, and full of wisdom too. "But … but what can I do?" Magnus stammered. "I'm no good at anything."

"That's not true, Magnus. You did well on the war trail, and I've no doubt you're going to be a fine warrior. You've also got more brains than both your brothers put together – I've seen you watching and listening while they chatter. You keep your own counsel. You know when to speak, and when to stay silent. So will you help me? Remember, if I am king I will need an heir, and I can choose who I please."

Magnus sat still for a moment, hardly able to believe what he had heard. How strange it felt to be there with his father talking of such important things! He thought of all the times when he had asked himself what his destiny might be, and now he knew. A sudden draught made the candles flicker, and Magnus shivered. He wondered if the ghost of his grandfather was there in the chamber with them too.

"I am yours to command, Father," Magnus said. "Do what you will with me."

And just like that, with a few words, he changed his life for ever.

THREE
BAD NEWS

MAGNUS'S FATHER MADE him promise to keep their conversation secret – "a wise man never shows his hand until he strikes, Magnus" – and Magnus knew that made sense. Far too much was at stake for him to go around talking about his father's plans. But for the next few days he felt as if he were walking on air, or as if he were a hero from one of the old tales poets sung in the hall on long winter evenings. Beowulf, perhaps, the great warrior who slew the monster Grendel and became a king.

The earl summoned Magnus to his chamber for more conversations, mostly about other claimants to the throne. King Sweyn of Denmark and King Harald of Norway were said to have their eyes on England, and so was Duke William of Normandy. He was a true descendant of the Vikings who had seized Normandy from the French two hundred years before. The Normans spoke French themselves now, but Duke William was just as hard and ruthless as any Viking. He was also much closer to England than Sweyn and Harald – Normandy was only a day's sailing away from Bosham.

There were gifts as well, the promised necklace for Gytha, a thick chain made of Welsh gold, the same for Gunhild. For Godwin and Edmund there were new war spears, two each. But for Magnus there was something far more special. Hakon and another housecarl came into the hall bearing a large box between them. They put it down on the rush-covered floor, and the earl stepped forward to open the lid.

"Your brothers already have good war gear, Magnus," he said. "But you went on the war trail last year in a borrowed mail shirt and helmet. It's time you had your own."

Then out of the box his father took the finest mail-shirt Magnus had ever seen and handed it to him. It flowed through his hands like steel water, its links shining in the firelight. There was a helmet as well, the surface and nose-guard inlaid with gold to form an image of a dragon's head. And there were three weapons, beautiful in their deadliness – a sword of the best Frankish craft, a dagger with a carved handle, a war axe with a shaft the length of his forearm and a blade like a great eagle's beak.

Magnus's father wanted to be sure the mail shirt and helmet fitted him, so Magnus put everything on and stood proudly before his family. His sisters squealed their approval, and his mother smiled and said he looked wonderful, although there was sadness in her face. But his brothers said nothing.

Godwin and Edmund sat staring at him with cold, hard eyes, their arms folded and their mouths shut tight.

They cornered him in a dark part of the hall later that evening. Godwin shoved him in the chest, pushing him back against the wall, the logs hard against his spine. "Tell me, little brother, why are you so special all of a sudden?" said Godwin, his eyes full of anger now. "And why is it that your gifts from Father are so much better than ours? They're fit for a prince, but we were only given a couple of spears each."

"And why are you spending so much time with Father?" said Edmund. He shoved Magnus in the chest too, and stood so close Magnus could feel his breath on his cheek, smell the meat Edmund had eaten earlier. "People might think you're being put ahead of us, and that wouldn't be right, would it, now?" Edmund went on. "We're older than you, which means we should come before you in everything."

Magnus very nearly told them the truth. He liked his brothers and they usually got on well. Of course

42

they bickered and lost their tempers with each other, as brothers do, but they always made friends afterwards. He couldn't break the promise he had made to their father, though, not even for them. And what would he say, anyway? How could he tell them they were right, they had been displaced?

"It isn't like that, honestly," he said at last. He wasn't used to lying, and the words sounded false even to him. "I don't know why Father is being so good to me…"

"Every dog has its day, boys," said a voice behind them. Their father stepped out of the shadows, a smile playing on his lips. "Things are going well for Magnus at the moment, Godwin, but it could be your day tomorrow. Or yours, Edmund."

"Oh, hello, Father," said Godwin, startled. Magnus could tell he was desperately trying to work out how much their father had heard. "We didn't see you there."

"Is that right?" said the earl, his voice soft. "Well, perhaps you should try to keep your wits about you – a good warrior is never caught unawares. And what were you talking about? It sounded as if you were having some kind of quarrel."

"A quarrel?" said Edmund, trying to look confused and innocent all at the same time. "No, we were just teasing our little brother – weren't we, Magnus?"

Magnus shrugged, and nodded. "I'm glad to hear it," said the earl. "We should stick together in times like these – remember, the family must always come first."

Godwin and Edmund mumbled their agreement, and their father talked to them for a while longer. But it was clear they wanted to escape, and he let them go.

"You did well, Magnus," he said once they were out of earshot. "But stand up to them next time. They will accept what is to come if you prove you deserve it."

"Yes, Father," said Magnus, wondering if he could ever be that strong.

The next morning a rider came with letters for the earl, and that afternoon Magnus was summoned once more. His father sat brooding over the same map. "How would you like to go and see your uncle Tostig, Magnus?" he said, looking up.

"I would like that very much, Father." Magnus smiled. Tostig was his favourite uncle, and he knew Tostig liked him too. At the age of seven, Magnus had been sent to live with Tostig as his foster-son for a year, as was the custom in noble families.

"Good," said his father. "Although this won't be just a family visit – I have an important task in mind for you. Tell me what you know about Northumbria."

Magnus stopped smiling and sat up straight. "I know that King Edward made Uncle Tostig the Earl of Northumbria a few years ago, and that he rules from the city of York, or Jorvik, as the Vikings called it. They ruled there for a long time."

"It's the key to Northumbria," said his father. "And Northumbria is the key to keeping England together. If we lose control of the North, Mercia might be next, and then the whole kingdom could fall apart before anyone can succeed Edward."

"But Uncle Tostig is strong, a great warrior. He wouldn't let that happen."

"Maybe not, but there is bad news from the North." The earl paused and glanced at a letter in front of him. "Something is wrong up there in York, yet my brother is too proud and stubborn to tell me what's been going on. I need you to find out."

"I won't let you down, Father." Magnus loved the idea that the first task he was to perform for his father would help his favourite uncle too.

"Good, that's settled," said the earl, looking pleased. "You will leave tomorrow with a half-troop of my housecarls. Hakon will be your second in command."

"Does that mean I'll be in charge?" Magnus felt his stomach twist into a knot.

"How else will you learn to be a leader of men?" said his father. "Besides, you are my son and a Godwin, and it would not be fitting for you to take a lesser place. Oh, and one more thing, Magnus – there's no need to tell your uncle why I'm sending you to see him. It would be best if you let him think it *is* just a family visit."

Magnus nodded. It was only later that he wondered why this should be.

The rest of the day was a whirl of preparation. There were more maps to look at, a route to be planned, supplies and weapons and armour to be packed. Magnus was soon very grateful to Hakon, who knew what to do and got on with it. Late that evening, a servant came to tell Magnus his mother wished to see him in her chamber. She sat wrapped in her blue gown, her eyes soft in the warm candlelight.

"I thought it best to bid you a mother's farewell tonight," she said, rising to kiss him. "You won't want me to do that in front of the housecarls tomorrow."

"I wouldn't mind," he said, smiling. "After all, you are my mother."

"But now you are entering the world of great men, where a mother's love cannot protect you," she said, that familiar look of sadness in her face. "I prayed for you last year when you were on the war trail, and I will pray for you again. I have some words of advice for you too. Be careful, Magnus. Things are not always what they seem. Sometimes the Godwins themselves can be their own worst enemies."

"What do you mean?" said Magnus, his voice small in the shadowy chamber. But she would say no more, and sent him off to his own chamber to sleep.

He lay awake for most of that night, brooding on her words.

FOUR
DARK BLOOD

THEY LEFT AT dawn the next day, the earl there to bid them farewell as they rode out through the gate.

Magnus led the column with Hakon by his side, twenty-five housecarls following, behind them a dozen spare mounts carrying their weapons and armour and

supplies. The track from the farm led over the hills, and by the time the sun was up properly they were well on their way, travelling northwards. Magnus set the pace, a steady trot – and continued to brood on what his mother had said.

He felt proud that his father had given him such a task and a half-troop of his own housecarls to lead. Magnus was determined to make a good job of it – but now he was confused. What had his mother meant? How could the Godwins be their own worst enemies? The family was doing fine, and Magnus was sure his father would sort out Uncle Tostig's problems... Eventually Magnus decided it had just been his mother's fears for him that had made her talk like that, and he put it out of his mind.

The journey was uneventful, at least to begin with. The lands they rode through were peaceful and prosperous, the people they encountered wary of armed men, but not terrified. On the first day they stopped at dusk to make camp beside a narrow stream. Magnus wondered if he should give orders, but he remembered from the war trail that warriors like these didn't need them. They fed and watered the horses, lit a fire and made a meal, sorted out who would stand watch and when.

"How long will it take to get to York, Hakon?" he said at last. They were sitting together by the fire, the rest of the men spread out in a circle around it, sparks floating in the coils of smoke that rose above them. A fox barked somewhere in the night.

"If we ride hard, maybe fifteen days. Longer if we don't."

"We'll be riding hard then. The sooner we arrive the better."

Hakon turned to him and raised an eyebrow. Magnus could see the red and yellow flames of the fire dancing in the housecarl's eyes. "So, this will be more than just a family visit, will it?" Hakon said quietly. "Is there anything you want to tell me, Magnus? It would be good to know what kind of trouble we'll be riding into."

"Why do you say that? It sounds as if you're expecting it."

"I always expect trouble, and I know that your

uncle has enemies in the North. I'm guessing the earl is sending you to find out how bad things really are."

"Is it so obvious?" Magnus felt his cheeks burning. He thought about what he had said that day, trying to recall if he had revealed anything. "What have you heard?" he said. "My father didn't mention any enemies."

"Did he not?" Hakon stared at him for a long moment, then he shrugged and turned away to stare into the flames again. "Well, I am only one of the earl's sworn men, and I have no right to speak of such matters."

Magnus tried for a while to get Hakon to say more, but the housecarl's face was closed and he refused to be drawn on the subject. Hakon only spoke when he wanted to, as Magnus well knew. It was frustrating – everybody seemed to know something about what was happening with Uncle Tostig, but nobody was willing to speak of it. The more Magnus brooded, the more he wished he knew himself what kind of trouble they were riding towards.

* * *

Four days later they splashed across a ford over the Thames and entered Mercia. The country was much the same as south of the river, and so were the people and their farms, although as Magnus and his men travelled north he noticed settlements were fewer and further between. By the tenth day ploughed fields began to give way to wild moors and hills, and another five days brought them to Northumbria, where they followed the Roman road that would take them the last few miles to York.

It was covered in dirt, but the old paving stones were beneath the soil and the road was wide and straight as an arrow. They kept moving northwards, the sun shining on a cloudless afternoon. After a while Magnus saw a dark smudge of smoke rising into the sky from somewhere ahead. Hakon had seen it too and reined in his horse. He peered into the distance, shielding his eyes from the sun with his hand.

"What is it, Hakon?" said Magnus, stopping beside him. "A forest fire?"

"No, I'd say that's a farm burning," said Hakon. "It might be raiders."

"Do you think so? What should we do?" said Magnus, the words tumbling out of his mouth before he could stop them. He felt his cheeks grow warm with shame in front of Hakon and the men. As their leader, he should *know* what to do.

"Make sure we're ready for whatever we find," Hakon said quietly. He glanced back at the spare mounts, then let his eyes fall on a couple of the men behind.

Magnus followed his gaze and understood what Hakon was telling him. "Right, we'll get armed before we go any further," Magnus said in as loud and bold a voice as he could. "Then I want you two men to scout ahead, find out what's happening."

"An excellent plan, my lord," said Hakon, his face serious, his eyes smiling.

They halted, unpacked their weapons and armour from the spare mounts, and quickly prepared themselves. Magnus put on his mail-shirt and helmet, checked his sword, tucked his axe in his belt. The scouts galloped off, one onto the moor to the left of the road, the other taking a track through the trees on the right. Hakon said to give them a good start, but eventually Magnus led the others – now a line of mail-clad warriors bristling with spear blades and shields – towards the smoke.

A mile or so down the road they came to another track. It led up a hill, straight towards the column of smoke, which now filled the sky before them. Magnus looked at Hakon, who nodded, and they took the track to the crest of the hill. Just before they got there both scouts returned from beyond it and stopped in front of them.

"Looks like a raid," said one. "But whoever it was is long gone."

Magnus spurred on his horse, rode up to the crest and paused. Below him was a wide valley with a stream running through it between rich green pastures. Someone had built a farmhouse in the heart of the valley, and a barn and byres, and circled them with a palisade. But now they were burnt-out ruins, their blackened timbers like the ribs of giant skeletons, the cold air filled with the reek of charred wood.

"Well, it seems they made a fight of it, anyway," Hakon said.

Magnus rode down to the five bodies that were lying in the farmyard. A trio of ravens had settled on them to peck at their flesh, and now the birds flew off with indignant squawks. Two of the dead were grown men, the others boys of a similar age to Magnus and his brothers. Each one had a hunting spear or wood-axe in his hand or lying nearby. All of them had the kind of wounds Magnus had seen on the war trail – limbs hacked off, stomachs pierced by spear thrusts, heads split open by sword or axe. Their dark blood lay in pools, seeping into the mud beneath them.

Magnus felt his stomach churn. His breakfast of porridge rose into his throat, the taste of bile strong in his mouth, and he leaned away from his horse to be sick. "Who did this, Hakon?" he said, wiping his mouth. "And where are the women?"

"Could have been some neighbours with a grudge," said Hakon, shrugging. "Could just as well have been raiders, a war-band passing through.

Maybe your uncle will be able to tell you. If they had any dead or wounded they must have taken them away when they left. And you know what happened to the women, Magnus."

Hakon was right. Magnus knew very well that they would find the bodies of the older women in the burnt farmhouse, and that any younger women and girls would have been taken to be sold as slaves. Magnus offered up a silent prayer for them, thinking of his mother and sisters.

"There is nothing we can do here," he said at last. "We ride on – to York."

The sun was sinking in a blaze of red over the hills when they arrived, and Magnus saw the city was ringed by the old Roman walls, although in many places they had been roughly repaired with stone. The wooden gates were shut, and a dozen warriors stared down from the battlements at the top of the tall gatehouse. One raised a war bow and fired an arrow that thumped into the ground in front of Hakon's mount.

"Now that's no way to welcome an important guest, is it, lads?" Hakon called out. "The lord Magnus, son of Harold Godwinson, has ridden a long way to visit his uncle Tostig. You'd better open those gates for him, and be quick about it."

There was a flurry of movement at the top of the gatehouse, and Magnus could hear men yelling. Moments later the gates slowly began to grind open.

Magnus spurred his horse forward into the city of York, Hakon at his side.

FIVE
BOUGHT MEN

 A WARRIOR STEPPED forward to stop them as they clattered beneath the gatehouse arch and into the street beyond. He was in mail shirt and helmet, a sword in a scabbard on his belt and a spear in his hand. Beyond him were a dozen more mail-shirted guards with spears and axes, two of them holding big war bows, barbed arrows notched and ready to fire.

Magnus halted his horse, Hakon staying close.

"Apologies for the arrow, my lord," said the warrior in Danish. His voice was friendly enough, but his eyes were cold and hard. "We've been having a bit of trouble with the locals and my lads get twitchy, especially after the sun goes down."

"Think nothing of it," said Magnus in the same tongue. Everyone in the Godwin family was brought up to speak Danish as well as they did English. His grandmother Gytha wouldn't have had it any other way. "Where can I find my uncle the Earl?"

"Why, in his palace, of course," said the warrior. "I sent one of my lads to tell him of your arrival. You just need to head down this street, cross the bridge, and—"

"I know where the palace is," Hakon said.

"Do you, now?" said the warrior, turning to look at Hakon with narrowed eyes. "So, you've been to Jorvik before, have you? What did you say your name was?"

"I didn't," said Hakon, spurring his horse on again, Magnus and the others behind him, the gatehouse guards staring silently at them as they rode past. The street was lined with stone-built Roman houses on both sides, although their roofs were thatched like country steadings, and more recent wooden dwellings were squeezed in any gaps. At the end of the street was a river with boats tied up on both banks – Magnus counted seven as they crossed the bridge, three of them longships.

Beyond the bridge was another street that took them past a big church with a tall, square bell tower and wooden doors twice the height of a man. Magnus realized it must be the church of York's archbishop, who was nearly as important as the Archbishop of Canterbury. There were many people around in this part of the city, but most hurried inside when they saw them coming, or just stared coldly. The sky was almost dark now, and shadows were creeping over the city. Magnus thought it felt like a place full of ancient ghosts, and a shiver crept up his spine.

They came at last to a second gatehouse, this one leading to a courtyard in front of another large building. It must once have had four storeys, but the top floor was missing, and a more recent roof of wood and thatch sat where it should have been. A line of warriors stood in front of the doorway, some of them holding torches. Hakon halted his horse and jumped down, and Magnus and the others did the same.

"What do you think, Hakon?" Magnus said quietly. "I've got a feeling they've had more than just a bit of trouble. It's almost as if the city is under siege."

"Yes, and they should never have let us in that easily," said Hakon. "I might have been lying. But then you can't expect bought men to have any brains."

"Bought? How could you tell? I thought they were my uncle's sworn men."

"Your uncle does not have any sworn men, Magnus. He is not like your father. Men do not serve Tostig out of love, but only for the gold and silver he pays them. I have met many bought men in my time. And killed my fair share as well."

Magnus felt a wave of anger at Hakon's words. This was not the Tostig he remembered, a strong, good man and loving foster-father. "Who are you to speak of my uncle that way?" he said. "He is a lord and you are nothing but a sworn man."

"I am your father's sworn man, Magnus," said Hakon. "Not your uncle's."

A young warrior interrupted them. "Earl Tostig bids me welcome you to his city of Jorvik, my lord," he said to Magnus. "Your men will be well taken care of. The earl awaits you in his great hall."

Magnus scowled at Hakon, but the housecarl shrugged and said no more. So Magnus tossed him his shield and followed the warrior into his uncle's palace.

The great hall was a long, wide chamber with a beamed ceiling and a central hearth, and it took up almost the building's entire bottom floor. There was no fire in the hearth, just grey ashes, but candles of all sizes stood around the ancient walls, or on the ledges of the high, shuttered windows, and they cast pools of warm yellow light that seemed to make the deep shadows in the corners even darker.

A group of guards stood at the far end, and Magnus could also see several priests in long black robes. Somebody was talking, the words English, the voice raised in anger. "What do you mean, you can't make them pay? That's what I pay *you* for. They're peasants, and you're supposed to be hardened warriors. Maybe I should send a few of your priests to do the job instead, Ealdred."

The young warrior pushed through the men, and Magnus followed, removing his helmet. Magnus had recognized the voice as that of his uncle, and now he saw Tostig sitting on a throne-like chair. His green tunic was of the finest cloth, and he had a heavy gold chain around his neck and gold and silver rings on his fingers. He was bigger and fairer than Harold, his hair and moustache almost corn-yellow – people often said Tostig was the most Danish-looking of all the Godwins. It had been three years since Magnus had seen him last, at a Godwin gathering, where Tostig had been his usual loud, cheerful self. Now he was scowling at the men in front of him.

He turned to Magnus and smiled, though, and leaped to his feet to grab him in a bear hug. "Magnus! Is it really you? I can't believe how much you've grown! You're practically a man! And what in God's name are you doing up here in the wild North?" Tostig partly released him, but left a steely arm slung round his shoulders. "Actually, you can tell me later – first I want you to help me convince these fools I'm right. They're supposed to give me advice, but all they do is argue with me."

"I hardly think so, my lord," somebody said. "We are merely trying to help."

Magnus looked at the man who had spoken. He was old, fifty winters or even more, and his hair was thin and grey. Like all priests and monks, his pale face was clean-shaven, but he was wearing the rich robes of a High-Churchman, a long blue silk gown with crosses embroidered on it, and a fine black cloak. He too wore a heavy chain around his neck, although his had a large gold cross hanging from it.

"Magnus, meet Ealdred, Archbishop of York," said Tostig.

Ealdred inclined his head to Magnus in greeting, and Magnus nodded. He knew most people would have knelt to kiss the ring of office the archbishop wore, but his father had taught him that was something a Godwin would never do.

"So, Magnus," Tostig went on, "will you help me?"

It was strangely unsettling to hear his uncle ask him the same question as his father. Magnus hesitated and looked uneasily round the circle of men, all of them now staring at him, waiting for his answer. "I will if I can, Uncle," he said.

"Good," said Tostig, nodding. "I think it's simple. You need money to run an earldom – you'd agree with that, wouldn't you, Magnus?"

"Of course," said Magnus, shrugging.

"And the money should come from the taxes paid by the people," said Tostig. "The taxes that I set as the Earl of Northumbria, their lord. That's fair enough, isn't it?" Magnus opened his mouth to answer, but Tostig kept talking, his voice rising again. He glared at the men in the room, his gaze clearly making them uncomfortable. "And if the people refuse to pay their taxes, then I have the right to make them."

"My lord, you know there is more to it…" Ealdred said softly.

Tostig let go of Magnus, strode over to the archbishop and stood looming over him. He was a head taller than Ealdred, but the archbishop didn't flinch. "There … is … *NOT*," Tostig said, the words hissing out of his mouth. "I am the rightful lord of the North, and I will not allow anyone to take my earldom from me, do you hear?"

"Times are hard and the people are unhappy, my lord," said Ealdred. "I'm sorry to say this, but you are making them hate you. The more farms your men burn, the more rebels you will have to face. You are doing your enemies' work for them."

Tostig said something in reply, but Magnus had stopped listening, his mind suddenly full of horror. So it had been his uncle's men who had burnt the farm he had seen earlier that day – and his uncle had clearly given the order.

"We will speak of this no more!" Tostig roared at last, silencing Ealdred. "You men will just have to do better, do you understand? Come, Magnus. You must be hungry. We will eat in my private chamber, where I don't have to look at these wretches."

Magnus glanced at Archbishop Ealdred, and their eyes met briefly across the hall. But Tostig was rapidly striding away, and Magnus turned to follow him.

He could hear the other men already whispering behind them.

SIX

BORN TO RULE

TOSTIG'S PRIVATE CHAMBER was a large room at the top of the palace. On one side was a bed covered with furs, and on the other was a wide window. The shutters were open, and Magnus could see the dark city laid out below, the dull glow of torches here and there like the last sparks of a

dying hearth-fire. Tostig helped Magnus out of his mail shirt and ordered the servants to bring food and drink. Magnus asked after his aunt, Tostig's wife Judith, and their sons, Skuli and Ketil, both younger than him.

"It's not safe here for my family," said Tostig, looking uneasy. "I've sent them to London, into the care of King Edward. I'll let them come back when things have settled down." He paused, then turned to Magnus and smiled. "I know why you've come to York, Magnus."

Magnus froze, a chunk of meat wrapped in bread halfway to his mouth. He had been worrying about this moment since he had left Sussex, wondering if he really could lie to his uncle and get away with it. Now it seemed Tostig had seen through him before he'd even had a chance to try.

"Your father and I haven't always been the best of friends," Tostig went on. "In fact, I'd say we've been rivals since we could barely walk. Did I ever tell you about the time he tried to drown me in the duck-pond at Bosham? It was our mother who saved me.

70

She gave your father such a beating! It almost turned his backside blue."

"I … I can imagine," said Magnus, unsure of why his uncle was suddenly talking about the past. But at least this was more like the Tostig he remembered than the raging lord of earlier. Magnus knew his father and Tostig had sometimes argued. It happened in all families, though, and it had never seemed to matter much, and both Harold and Tostig got on well with their other brothers, Gyrth and Leofwine.

"But I have to hand it to him," said Tostig, smiling now. "This is all part of your education, isn't it? Harold has sent you here so I can teach you how to rule an earldom. Well, maybe he didn't realize it, but you couldn't have come at a better time. This is where you'll learn that ruling isn't easy."

Magnus relaxed, relieved he wouldn't have to lie after all, and crushed a twinge of guilt. He was doing this for his uncle as well as his father, wasn't he? "I think I already knew that," he said, and put the meat and bread in his mouth.

"But you don't know just how bad it can be."

Tostig went over to the window and looked down on the city. "I tried to be the kind of ruler people love," he said softly. "But there are those in the North who have always wanted me to fail – the old Viking families who once ruled in Northumbria, and that evil wretch Edwin of Mercia and his foul brother Morcar. They have turned the people's hearts against me…"

The names were familiar to Magnus from conversations with his father. Edwin was Earl of Mercia, a powerful man with plenty of ambition. He had struck up an alliance with Gruffudd of Gwynedd and married his own sister Aldgyth off to him, but Gruffudd was dead, killed by Magnus's father two years ago. So perhaps Edwin no longer favoured the Godwins. It seemed he had clearly turned his attention to Northumbria now – and if he seized control of the North he would become a real threat.

"But isn't the archbishop right?" said Magnus. "Aren't you making things worse? I've seen what your men are doing. We passed a burnt farm on our way here."

Tostig turned round, his face suddenly hard. "What would you have me do, Magnus? I am the earl, yet the people will not obey me."

"I don't know, Uncle. But surely there must be some other way."

"Only the way of the weak. Ealdred wants me to meet Edwin and Morcar and the rest to sort out our differences, but that's not what a great ruler does. The tide will turn in my favour, I'm certain of it. A ruler always has to stay strong."

"Even when that means killing your own people?"

Magnus fell silent, worried he had gone too far. Tostig stared at him for a moment – and then he laughed. "I can see you've still got plenty of learning to do, Magnus. We are the Godwins, and they are peasants. We are born to rule over others, although occasionally we have to kill a few to make them understand that. And we always win, even when the odds are stacked against us. I will show you how it's done."

Magnus tried to smile, but he wasn't sure he wanted to know.

* * *

Over the next two days Magnus spent a lot of time with his uncle. Tostig took him on a tour of the city, showed him how well the walls were defended and introduced him to his commanders, including the man who had spoken at the gatehouse, whose name turned out to be Gisli. Everywhere they went, Tostig was loud and cheerful, laughing and slapping backs, keeping his anger only for those who brought him bad news.

It wasn't till the third day that Magnus had a chance to check on his own men. They were doing weapons practice in a courtyard beneath a warm sun, training in pairs with sword and shield. Hakon was standing at the side observing.

"Glad to see you're keeping them busy," Magnus said, smiling. He felt a little nervous, remembering how angry he had been with Hakon at the gatehouse when they had arrived. Things had changed since then, and however much Magnus hated the idea, he had to admit that Hakon was probably right about his uncle Tostig.

Hakon turned to look at Magnus – and returned

his smile. "There's not much else to do," he said. "We went to a few of the taverns, but I've been to burials that were more cheerful. The people aren't very friendly."

"I can understand that," said Magnus. "They probably think we're the same as my uncle's bought men, and that gives them good reason to hate us."

Magnus told Hakon what he had discovered – he felt he would burst if he didn't tell someone, and he trusted the housecarl. Hakon listened in silence, rubbing his chin thoughtfully. "Edwin and Morcar, you say," he murmured at last. "That would explain a lot. They're more dangerous than a barrel full of snakes, and trickier too."

"But is burning farms the right way to deal with them?"

"That depends on whether it works or not. I've seen it tried by other lords in trouble. If you burn enough farms and kill enough people, the rest might start to think it would be better to do what you want. But dead farmers don't pay taxes. And it's dangerous to rely only on bought men. What if Edwin and Morcar offer them more money to switch sides? Then your uncle would be finished."

Magnus left him after a while, and found a quiet spot where he could think, a small square with a great oak at its heart. He sat on a bench beneath the tree and went over everything in his mind. He was sure his father would want Tostig to defeat Edwin and Morcar, and if Hakon was right, then maybe Tostig didn't really have much choice in how to fight them. Magnus might not like what Tostig was doing, but what if the tide was truly turning in his favour?

There was only one way to find out, Magnus realized. He should escape from this miserable city, go and talk to the people in the farms and villages, ask them what they thought. That's what his father would expect him to do, he was certain. He hurried back to the palace, deciding that he would say his men needed proper exercise, so he would like to take them on a short patrol into the countryside.

"I don't see why not," said Tostig. "The more patrols we send out the better. But I can't let you go with just a handful of men. That would be too dangerous

– your father would never forgive me if I returned you to him without that handsome Godwin head of yours. You'd better take fifty of my men along with you as well."

Magnus tried to argue, but his uncle was stubborn and wouldn't listen.

At dawn the next morning Magnus and Hakon and the housecarls were sitting on their horses in the street that led to the gatehouse. They were ready, sunlight flashing off their helmets and spear blades and the iron bosses of their shields. The horses snickered impatiently, as keen as their riders to move out. But Tostig's men were taking ages to get organized, most of them yawning, barely awake. At last they were ready too, and their commander – Gisli – trotted his horse over to Magnus.

"Morning, lads!" he said with a grin, speaking in Danish. "As this is your patrol, it's only fair that you should take the lead. My men and I will be right behind you."

"I'd rather you were in front," growled Hakon.

"Where I can see you."

"It doesn't matter, Hakon," said Magnus. He spurred his horse forwards, and they clattered out through the open gates. The road stretched ahead towards the sun.

But Magnus could see a mass of dark clouds gathering in the distance.

SEVEN

HAIL OF ARROWS

THEY RODE WEST into broken country where small farms clung to rocky hillsides. People ran as soon as they saw them coming, mothers grabbing their children and shutting themselves in the farmhouses, the men reaching for the weapons they clearly kept close at hand when they

were working in the fields. Magnus saw the loathing in their faces – and soon realized there was no point speaking to them.

Late in the afternoon they came to a village, a poor-looking place in a valley, most of the houses little more than rough huts. They rode into the centre and halted. The thin, ragged villagers stared at them, children clutching their mothers' legs, their eyes wide with fear. Several of Gisli's men jumped off their horses and strode up to the huts, shoving people out of the way, kicking doors open and pushing their way inside.

"Where are you, Osric?" Gisli shouted in Danish. "Come and talk to me."

An old man emerged from one of the huts and stood looking up at the warriors on their horses – the village elder, Magnus assumed. A few wisps of white hair clung to his head and chin, and he was even skinnier than everyone else in the village.

"We have paid your taxes," the elder said, also in Danish, although with the accent of someone more used to speaking English. "We have nothing else to give you."

80

"Oh, I doubt that," said Gisli, laughing. "I'll bet you've got all sorts of treasures hidden in these filthy hovels. We'll soon find out, anyway."

"You will do as you wish," the elder said bitterly. "We can't stop you."

"Cheer up, Osric," said Gisli. "This is a friendly visit – isn't it, my lord?"

He turned to Magnus and grinned. Elsewhere in the village there was a crash and somebody screamed. "It doesn't sound like it to me," said Magnus, tight-lipped.

"Oh, that's just one of the lads having a bit of fun," said Gisli.

"Tell him his fun is over," said Magnus. "We are finished here."

They took a different route back to York, a quick one, according to Gisli. The sky was filled with dark clouds now, and the afternoon grew dim and murky, the shadows lengthening, making it feel as if night was almost upon them. Magnus was barely aware of his surroundings – he couldn't stop thinking of the terrified villagers, and how he had hated seeing Gisli and his men treating them that way. Hakon rode up close beside him, breaking into his thoughts.

"Keep your shield high, Magnus. I don't like the look of this place."

Magnus glanced round. They were riding through a narrow, forested valley, steep slopes on both sides. Gisli and his men were in front, strung out loosely along the track, the housecarls riding in pairs behind them. As he looked, Magnus caught a glimpse of shapes moving swiftly between the trees. Suddenly he heard a thrumming sound, and an arrow thwacked into the throat of the bought man just ahead of him. The man toppled off his horse, blood spurting from the wound.

"*AMBUSH!*" Hakon yelled, and arrows thwacked into Gisli's men and some of their horses. Magnus felt one fly past his face, the feathers brushing his helmet's cheek-guard. He heard arrows thumping into the shields of his housecarls, Gisli shouting, a horse squealing in pain as it thrashed on the ground.

Then waves of warriors charged down the slopes screaming war cries, and Magnus barely had time to draw his sword before they reached him.

Two ran straight at him, both carrying spears and round shields bearing the image of a double-headed eagle. The first warrior jabbed his spear upwards, and Magnus deflected the blade with his shield. Before he could recover, the second thrust at him, ramming his spear hard into the shield, knocking Magnus clean off his horse. He landed on the muddy track, and rolled aside just before the first man's spear stabbed into the ground where his head had been.

Magnus scrambled to his feet, still holding his sword and shield. The two warriors stood together now, facing him, one holding his spear high as if he were about to throw it, the other keeping his low for another thrust. The chaos of battle swirled around the three of them, blades rising and falling, shapes moving, men shouting. But for Magnus the world had shrunk to the eyes of the two men staring at him from beneath the rims of their helmets,

and he knew he had to strike first or die.

So he leaped forward, screaming as loudly as he could, and crashed his shield into that of the warrior on the left, pushing him back. He swung his sword at the other man too, making him recoil. But they steadied themselves and advanced again, jabbing at Magnus with their spears, moving apart so he would leave himself open to one of them. As he had been taught, Magnus gave ground with his shield up, his heart pounding, his eyes flicking between the two men who wanted to kill him.

Suddenly Hakon appeared at his right shoulder. "With me, Magnus," he said, his voice calm, and the housecarl stepped forward, hooking the blade of an axe over the shield rim of the nearest warrior in front of them, pulling it down to expose him. Magnus knew what he was expected to do, and swung his sword, feeling the blade slice deep into flesh till it jarred against bone. Hakon hooked the other man's feet from under him with the axe, then smashed it into his neck. The dark blood spurted, and the warrior coughed and gurgled his life away.

"Are you all right, Magnus?" said Hakon, turning to him. "Any wounds?"

"I'm fine," said Magnus. He stared at the bodies, their faces frozen in agony. His stomach churned and a foul taste filled his mouth, but he wouldn't let himself be sick, not when the battle was still going on. He looked round and saw that his housecarls had dismounted and formed a shield-wall, spears poking through like the spikes of a giant hedgehog. There were corpses heaped in front of them, but his house-carls weren't fighting anyone.

"We were too strong for these northern wolves," said Hakon, seeing his puzzled expression. "They were after easier prey, and your uncle has provided it."

Magnus looked up the track and saw what he meant – Tostig's men were surrounded by the ambushers. Some of them had managed to remain on their horses, but most were on foot, struggling to form a defensive wall. Magnus saw Gisli cut down, and couldn't help feeling a surge of dark satisfaction at the sight.

"I suppose we ought to save them," said Magnus. "Not that I want to."

"Then let's help slaughter them instead," said Hakon with a grin.

Magnus sighed. "You know I can't allow that, Hakon. Come on…"

But the ambushers broke off and melted away as soon as they saw the housecarls approaching. Magnus felt he was being watched, and raised his eyes to the end of the valley. On a ridge two riders were outlined against the sky.

They turned and slowly rode off, vanishing into the gathering gloom.

Tostig was furious. He raged up and down the great hall, yelling at his commanders and Archbishop Ealdred. "You see how bold Edwin has become? He doesn't even bother to conceal his foul treachery any more. The double-headed eagle is the symbol of Mercia, so they were *his* men, attacking *my* men in *my* earldom. Well, the swine has gone too far this time!" Then he stormed out, followed by almost everyone – except for Magnus, Hakon and Archbishop Ealdred.

"This cannot go on, Magnus," Ealdred said quietly. "Things are far worse now than when I wrote to your father. Earl Tostig is losing, but he refuses to admit it."

Magnus remembered the letter his father had brooded over. He wondered how many other letters Ealdred had written to his father, and what they had said.

"Be careful how you speak of my lord's uncle, *priest*," said Hakon, practically spitting out the last word, hand on the hilt of his sword. "Earl Tostig is a great warrior, and I doubt you've ever held a sword in your life."

Magnus looked at Hakon, startled by the venom in the housecarl's voice – it sounded as if he wanted to kill the archbishop. And after Hakon's comments about Tostig at the gatehouse, Magnus was surprised to hear him speak well of his uncle.

"That's as may be," the archbishop said calmly. "I know when a man is following the wrong path, though. Speak to your father, Magnus. He must deal with this, and he must do it soon. Time is running out in the North for Earl Tostig Godwinson."

The next day Magnus left York with his men, heading south.

EIGHT
ON THORNEY ISLAND

HAKON INSISTED THEY ride fully armed, even if it did mean the horses grew tired more quickly. Magnus didn't argue. He had been in one ambush on his trip to the North, and he had no desire to experience another. In the afternoon of the first day they saw riders on a distant hill, a dozen warriors shadowing them. That night Hakon found an old Roman watchtower to camp in, its upper floors gone but its walls solid.

Magnus sat by the fire they had made on the flagstones inside the tower, stars twinkling in the square of dark sky above them. They had posted guards, and the rest of the men were taking their ease, quietly talking, some sleeping, like Hakon beside him. But Magnus couldn't relax, and stared into the flames, dwelling on what he had seen in the North, trying to make up his mind what to say to his father.

It should have been easy. He could simply report that Tostig had got himself into a terrible mess, and tell his father what Edwin was plotting, although Magnus had a feeling Ealdred had already made his father aware of all that in his letter. Magnus could add detail, and pass on Ealdred's message about time running out, of course. But anybody else could have done as much. So his father must have sent him to York for a different reason – and suddenly Magnus realized what it was.

The whole thing was a test of whether he could be his father's heir, a son who would one day be a king. His father wanted him to do more than simply report back on what was happening in the North – he wanted Magnus to work out what they should *do*, to show he could think about problems and tactics and come up with answers. But that was hard, especially as he still didn't understand part of it.

"Wake up, Hakon," he said, nudging the house-carl with his boot. "I need to ask you something. Do you think King Edward knows what Edwin is doing?"

"Probably," Hakon said without opening his eyes. "The king's court is full of priests, and Ealdred is bound to have friends among them. People say he is as thick as thieves with Stigand, the Archbishop of Canterbury, the king's favourite."

"So why doesn't the king stop Edwin? He made my uncle Earl of Northumbria, and Edwin Earl of Mercia. Surely he doesn't want his earls to fight each other?"

Hakon sighed and opened his eyes. "He's a weak

king, Magnus, only interested in praying. He'll let the earls do what they please so long as whoever ends up as top dog stays loyal to him. And gives him plenty of gold so he can build more churches."

"I have another question," Magnus said. "How many housecarls would my uncle need to defeat Edwin? I mean properly, so he wouldn't be a threat any more."

"Your father has a thousand," said Hakon. "But five hundred should do it."

"Would you fight for my uncle? If he got rid of his bought men, that is."

"I am your father's sworn man, and I do whatever he bids me. So yes, I would fight for Tostig if that was your father's wish. Can I go back to sleep now?"

"Only if you tell me why you stood up to Ealdred for my uncle like that."

"Because it's true, your uncle is a great warrior, even if he is making a mess of things. And I hate priests. They're supposed to be good, but most are full of lies and just as greedy for gold and power as other men. Sleep well, Magnus."

In fact, Magnus slept better that night than he had done for many days. He knew what he was going to say now, and he was sure his father would agree.

The warriors shadowing them disappeared once Magnus and his men crossed back into Mercia, and the rest of the ride was as quiet as the journey to the North had been. After fifteen days they entered the courtyard of the Godwin farm – only to discover Earl Harold was no longer there. He had been summoned by King Edward not long after they had set out for York, and had left word that they should follow him.

Four days later Magnus led his men along the last stretch of the road to Thorney Island, the site of King Edward's palace. It was raining steadily, clouds hanging like giant sodden fleeces above their heads, and they were soaked. A wooden gate barred their way onto the bridge across the narrow tributary that separated the island from the north bank of the Thames. But it was guarded by more of his father's housecarls, who recognized Magnus and Hakon and waved them through.

Magnus had been to Thorney Island with his father several years ago. King Edward's palace was the same as he remembered, the hall even bigger than the one at the Godwin farm, a host of lesser buildings clustered around it. But since Magnus's last visit the king had ordered the building of a vast new church to replace the island's old abbey, and it was almost finished. Thorney was a few miles west of London, a city even bigger than York. People had started calling St Paul's – London's largest church – the East Minster, and the king's new church the West Minster, or Westminster Abbey.

Magnus sent his men off to get dry and fed, while he and Hakon made their way to the hall down a muddy street, past a tavern, a big smithy, and the huts of King Edward's servants. Rain dripped off the thatched roofs, and there were so many big puddles Magnus thought it was almost as if the island was sinking into the river. At last they left their horses with the housecarls guarding the hall's great entrance, and went inside.

The hall was enormous, its giant roof-beams

impossibly high. Grey, watery light seeped in through the tall windows along the side walls. Magnus and Hakon walked its length, their steps echoing off the stone floor, and passed nobles and priests huddled together, whispering. Hakon scowled, and most stepped backwards, giving him plenty of room, although a few stared at him with contempt. *We are the ones who rule here, not you lowly warriors,* their sneers seemed to say.

King Edward was at the far end of the hall, sitting on his throne. Magnus was shocked to see how ill the king looked. He was old, but he was deathly pale too, his cheeks sunken, his eyes red and rheumy beneath the circle of fine gold he wore on his wrinkled brow. His tunic was simple, but made of the best cloth, and a heavy gold cross hung on a chain round his thin neck.

Earl Harold was speaking to the king, leaning in very close to whisper into his ear.

Then the earl spotted Magnus, and gestured for him to come forward. Magnus knelt before the king and bowed his head.

"You remember my son Magnus, my lord?" said the earl, stepping back from the throne. "He has just returned from visiting his uncle Tostig in the North."

"Your son, you say?" The king spoke in a whisper. "You Godwins all look alike to me, and there are so many of you. But I am very fond of Tostig. How is he?"

"He is … well, my lord," said Magnus, glancing at his father. Suddenly the king started to cough, his thin chest heaving, and monks fussed around him.

"I fear we are tiring you, my lord," said the earl. "May we take our leave?"

King Edward nodded and waved them away, still coughing, his face red. The earl led Magnus and Hakon outside to a garden beside the wide river. He stopped by an ancient oak and turned to face Magnus, Hakon hanging back. The rain had stopped but a cool breeze ruffled the water.

"So, my brother is well, is he?" said the earl. "Tell me more, Magnus."

It didn't take long for Magnus to make his report. He told his father what he had seen and heard, leaving nothing out, and said that Tostig would certainly lose his earldom unless they helped him. "He needs more men, Father, real warriors, not the cowards he pays to burn farms. Hakon reckons five hundred of your housecarls could easily beat Edwin's men. Then we Godwins will keep control of Northumbria."

The earl looked at him for a moment, then smiled and squeezed his shoulder. "Well done, Magnus," he said. "I will think about all that you have told me."

Magnus smiled, but in his heart he had hoped for more.

NINE

TEST OF STRENGTH

MAGNUS SPENT THAT night with the off-duty
housecarls in the Thorney barracks. He brooded

on what his father
had said, and found
it hard to sleep. Had
he passed his father's
test? He had hoped
the earl would agree
with him, and give
an immediate order

for five hundred of the housecarls to ride North and save Tostig. Magnus dozed off eventually, although his dreams were full of blades and blood and corpses.

"Wake up, Magnus," said Hakon, shaking him. "Your father wants to see you."

Magnus opened his eyes, only to be dazzled by light flooding into the barracks from the high windows along its walls. Then Hakon's words sank in and Magnus sprang from his bed. He pulled on his boots and hurried out, trying to buckle on his sword belt as he ran. Suddenly he stopped, and turned to Hakon, who was waiting in the barracks doorway looking amused. "Where will I find my father, Hakon?"

"Not in that direction," said Hakon. "You'd better follow me."

Hakon took Magnus back to the king's hall. They walked down dark, narrow passages, coming at last to a large room. A dozen scribes – most of them monks – sat at tables working on piles of documents. Earl Harold sat at another table writing a letter. After a moment the earl signed the letter, stamped the wax seal with his signet ring, and handed it to a housecarl, who hurried away.

"Well, Magnus, you'll be pleased to know that I'll be riding north today," said the earl. "You were right, something needs to be done as soon as possible."

"Thank you, Father," said Magnus. "I'm sure my uncle Tostig will be relieved when he sees you riding into York at the head of five hundred men."

"That won't be happening just yet, Magnus. I need to talk to some other people before I decide what to do. There are many things to take into account."

"But you will help Uncle Tostig, won't you?" said Magnus, puzzled.

"Don't worry, it will all be dealt with…" His father paused for an instant, his face serious. But then he smiled. "Hakon tells me you handled yourself well in the fight you had in the North," he went on. "He says you might even have the makings of a leader. So I'm putting you in charge of a full troop of housecarls while you're here on Thorney. Do you think you could lead fifty men in battle, Magnus?"

"I … I would do my best, Father," said Magnus.

He should have known his father would ask Hakon about him. The housecarl had served under many troop leaders in his time, so he knew what he was talking about. Magnus felt glad he had come up to scratch – this *must* mean that he had passed his father's test.

"I could ask no more of any man," said Earl Harold. "Hakon will explain your duties to you. Now leave me. I have much to do before I set out."

The Earl rode north at dawn the next day, before Magnus had a chance to bid him farewell. It was high summer, and Magnus wouldn't see him again till the autumn.

Over the next few weeks Magnus discovered that being a troop leader was rather more complicated than he had imagined. There were duty rosters to work out, training to supervise, problems to solve. The housecarls were fine warriors, but sometimes they drank too much in the island's taverns and got into fights with each other, or with the sworn men of other lords. Magnus had to sit in judgement on the wrongdoers, some of them seasoned warriors more than twice his age.

He always took Hakon's advice on what punishments to give. Usually it was stopping their pay for a while, although that didn't really bother them. As Hakon said, nobody became a housecarl for the money, even if Earl Harold was a generous man. They did it to serve their lord, to fight for him and win glory and fame. And the oath a sworn man took bound him to one thing above all – to die for his lord. When a lord fell on the field of battle, his housecarls died with him, or lived in shame.

A better punishment was extra guard duty in the king's hall, with its pall of sickness and gloom. They all hated it, Magnus included. The hall never seemed to empty, the clusters of nobles and priests whispering and plotting and glaring at each other day and night, a crowd of ghouls waiting for Edward to die. Whatever you thought of the king – and the more Magnus saw of Edward, the less he liked him – he was still a man, and it seemed terrible to be so hated at the end of his life.

But they all enjoyed guard duty on the bridge, deciding who was allowed onto the island. There was a constant stream of traffic – nobles and priests to see the king, servants and slaves to work for him, carts arriving full of supplies and leaving empty. Magnus and his men checked everything, and he revelled in the sense of power it gave him. Everyone who came to the gate had to do as he said, whoever they were.

"Watch out, lads," said Hakon one dull afternoon. "These two look like trouble."

Magnus saw his brothers Godwin and Edmund approaching the gate, their cloaks travel-stained, their horses plodding wearily. Magnus glanced at Hakon, who smiled. Then Magnus nodded to the men to open the gate. He stepped out and held up a hand.

"Halt in the name of King Edward!" he said. "Who comes to Thorney?"

His brothers reined in their horses. "Is that you, Magnus?" said Godwin, peering down at him. "Be a good little brother and get out of our way, will you?"

"We've been on the road for five days and we're tired, so hurry up," said Edmund.

Magnus stared at him and didn't step back. "I say again – who comes to Thorney? You must give me your names and state your business here."

Godwin laughed. "Come on, Magnus, what are you playing at?"

"Playing?" said Magnus, his eyes locked on Godwin's now. "This is no game for children. I am the leader of the king's gate guard, and I can let no man through who will not tell me his name and say what business he has on Thorney Island."

"This is ridiculous," said Edmund. "Tell him to stop being stupid, Hakon."

"I cannot do that," said Hakon, shrugging. "He is lord and master here."

There was silence for a moment, and Magnus knew the housecarls behind him were enjoying this test of his strength. Godwin and Edmund looked at each other, and finally gave in. "We are Godwin and Edmund Haroldsson, here to pay our respects to the king, and also to meet our uncles Gyrth and Leofwine," snapped Godwin. "Is that good enough for you?"

"I suppose it will do," said Magnus. He knew he could make some remark now to belittle them further in front of Hakon and the housecarls, but that would probably risk turning them into real enemies. They were his brothers, and he wanted them on his side. So he grinned instead. "Had you worried there for a while, didn't I?" he said. "Welcome to Thorney! It's good to see you, my brothers."

There was laughter from Hakon and the housecarls, the kind that eases tensions, and the anger drained from his brothers' faces. "You think you're funny, do you?" said Godwin, smiling. "Maybe we should wipe that grin off your face."

"You're welcome to try," Magnus said, shrugging and grinning even more.

Magnus took them to the barracks and helped them settle in. He was still a little wary of them to begin with, wondering if their old friendship was truly restored, but he soon knew that it was. He asked how things were at home, and briefly told them about his trip to the North. Then he asked why they were meeting their uncles.

"Father sent a messenger to say we were to join their housecarls," said Edmund. "Me with Gyrth's, Godwin with Leofwine's. They're coming here to collect us."

"Did the messenger say what Father was doing?" asked Magnus.

"No," said Godwin. "Just that he was in Mercia."

"Mercia?" said Magnus, surprised. "I thought he was going to York."

"There was no mention of that," said Edmund.

Magnus said no more, but his mind was whirring.

TEN

A LONE RIDER

HARVEST TIME CAME and went and summer passed into autumn, the days growing shorter and

the nights cooler. Magnus still had no word from his father, and worry about what was happening in the North began to gnaw away at him. He had learned to ignore most of the rumours that always buzzed round King Edward's court. But there was constant talk of Tostig now, and even if Magnus only believed a tiny part of what he heard, things were clearly getting worse for his uncle.

Magnus tried not to think about it, concentrating on being a good troop leader instead. He had other distractions, chief among them the chance to see members of the wider Godwin clan. His uncles Gyrth and Leofwine arrived on Thorney a few days after his brothers. They were big, broad-shouldered, fair-haired men with hard Godwin faces and loud voices, more like Tostig than his father. They talked a lot and drank even more, although they never seemed to get drunk.

Grandmother Gytha lived in London, and when she discovered that so many of her descendants were on Thorney Island she demanded they visit her. Magnus and Hakon and his brothers and uncles rode there one chilly morning, entering at the great gate in the western wall. London had wide streets and bustling crowds, and Magnus thought it was far more impressive than York.

Grandmother Gytha's house was in the heart of the city. She was waiting for them in the enormous main room, and Magnus was pleased to see that she was the same as ever – tall and striking, her face framed by stone-grey hair, her cheekbones like the blades of axes, her eyes like shards of blue ice. She barked orders in Danish at her servants, who were clearly terrified of her.

"When are you going to learn to speak English, Grandmother?" Magnus said in Danish, smiling at her. His grandmother had lived in England most of her life, more than fifty winters all told, and yet she had always refused to speak the language of the Saxons, although everybody knew that she could understand it very well.

"English is for slaves and dogs," she said, airily dismissing it with a wave of her hand. "In our family we speak Danish, the tongue of warriors and kings. Now I want to hear everybody's news, and it had better be interesting. You first, Gyrth."

"Well, I don't know where to start," said Gyrth. "So much has happened..."

Both Gyrth and Leofwine did their best, but their news was the usual stuff of families – new babies, sicknesses suffered and recovered from, the death of an old servant she might have remembered. Godwin and Edmund talked about themselves, briefly mentioned their sisters – Gytha had a soft spot for her namesake – but they soon dried up. Magnus could see that his grandmother wasn't impressed.

"I hope you've got something more exciting to tell me, Magnus," she said.

"He should have," said Edmund. "He went to see Uncle Tostig in York."

"Did he now?" said Gytha. "So what kind of mess has Tostig got himself into this time? He's my handsomest son, but he's also the most rash and headstrong."

Once again Magnus found himself at the centre of a circle of faces, his family staring, waiting for him to start talking. It would have been easy in the past, but he knew his father would want him to be careful what he said, even to those he was related to by blood. So he repeated what he had told his brothers about Edwin and Morcar and the people not paying their taxes. But he hadn't told Godwin and Edmund how bad things were in the North, and he didn't go into any more detail now.

"He's being modest, Grandmother," said Godwin, punching him in the shoulder.

"Tell her about the fight you got into, Magnus, and how you killed a man."

"I only did what I was supposed to," said Magnus, his cheeks burning. "I'd probably be dead if it wasn't for Hakon," he said, glancing at the housecarl, who gave his usual shrug. "And I'm sure there's nothing to worry about, Grandmother," Magnus added. "My father has gone North to sort things out."

"That's good," said his grandmother. "I asked Tostig's wife to visit me when he first sent her to the king, and she did nothing but cry and upset those boys of hers. So I won't have her here any more. She should have shown more backbone and stayed with her husband, anyway. I've a good mind to pack her off back to where she came from – Flanders, wasn't it? Why, she can barely speak any Danish at all!"

"She was probably crying because you frightened

her half to death, Mother," said Leofwine, grinning. "You don't know how fierce you are."

"Oh, I think I do," she said, and scowled. "It's why I've survived this long."

They laughed, and she gave them a wintry smile. "Tell me, Grandmother, where is my aunt Edith, the queen?" said Magnus. "Shouldn't she be here with the king?"

"Don't talk to me about her," said Gytha, her smile vanishing. "She spends most of her time in some dreadful abbey miles from here. I can't blame her for not wanting to be with Edward, but she's letting the family down with all that praying. I don't know why she bothers. It didn't turn her husband into the kind of man who could give her sons, did it? Still, one day soon this land might have a proper king again."

"It sounds as if you know who that will be," said Magnus, still laughing.

"It should be your father, of course," she said. "In fact, I can't understand why Harold doesn't just cut Edward's scrawny throat and be done with it. We all know it would be a mercy for the sickly old fool, and for the rest of us as well."

"Hush, Grandmother, you shouldn't say such things." Magnus glanced round, but there were no servants in the room with them. His uncles and brothers were sniggering, and there was a faint smile on Hakon's lips too. Magnus rolled his eyes as if to say, *Don't listen, she's only trying to shock*. But then he realized his grandmother was frowning, and staring at him with those icy-blue eyes.

"Why not?" she snapped. "There are plenty of people who agree with me."

Magnus stopped smiling. It was clear that she had meant every word.

A few days later Gyrth and Leofwine left Thorney, taking Godwin and Edmund with them. The weather turned blustery and cold, and one morning when Magnus arrived for duty on the bridge, the muddy ruts in front of the gate glittered with a silvery frost. Hakon ordered the men to fetch braziers from the stores, and soon they had fires going.

After a while they heard hoofbeats, and Magnus saw a lone rider fast approaching the gate. Magnus stepped forward and held his hand up, and the rider brutally reined in his horse. It reared upwards, its eyes wild, then crashed its hooves to the ground. Both man and beast were panting heavily, the man's face deathly pale, his cloak and tunic splattered with mud, his mount covered in a sheen of sweat.

"Halt in the name of the king!" said Magnus. "Who comes to Thorney?"

"A messenger, and I bring evil news from the North," the man replied.

Magnus felt his blood go cold. He recognized the man. "You're one of my uncle Tostig's men, aren't you?" he said. "What has happened?"

"My message is for the ears of the king alone. Will you let me pass?"

The messenger stared down at him, his face hard, and Magnus could see there was no point in trying to make him talk. So he stepped aside, and the messenger spurred his horse through the gate, then galloped away towards the king's hall.

"Take over here, Hakon," said Magnus. "I need to find out what's going on."

Magnus ran after the messenger, his mind churning with dark thoughts, fears for his uncle, and for his father too. At the hall, two of the housecarls on door duty were struggling to bring the messenger's horse under control as it reared and snorted, its saddle now empty. Magnus hurried inside and pushed past anyone who got in his way, ignoring their curses.

King Edward was sitting on his throne, the messenger kneeling before him. As usual there were several priests near the throne too, among them one Magnus had come to know – Stigand, Archbishop of Canterbury. He was an old man, older even than Edward, his hair white and his face wrinkled. But he stood tall and straight-backed in his rich, embroidered robes, and his eyes glittered with sharpness.

"Ah, you're the Godwin boy who went to see poor Tostig, aren't you?" said the king, turning to Magnus. "You'd better hear what this messenger has to say."

"Are you sure, my lord?" said the messenger. The king nodded, and the messenger turned to Magnus.

"Edwin attacked York and many of Lord Tostig's men went over to him. The people of the city rose against Tostig too, and slaughtered most of the rest."

"What about Tostig?" said Magnus. "Did he get away?"

"I don't know. He was still in the palace when he sent me south."

Magnus turned and strode out of the hall, his fists clenched.

ELEVEN
LOST SOULS

IT TOOK HAKON a long time to calm Magnus down. He wanted to ride North with his troop and save Tostig, or find his father so they could save Tostig together, or do anything rather than just sit there on Thorney. "Your father won't want you to go off on some wild rescue bid and get yourself killed, Magnus," the housecarl said at last, his face stern. "The earl will be back soon, I'm sure. Better to wait till then."

Magnus knew Hakon was right, but waiting was hard. Within a few days new rumours were swirling round the king's court. According to one, Tostig had been caught in the palace and beheaded by Edwin himself. Others said he had escaped and made his way to Wales, or Ireland, or Denmark. There were rumours about Edwin, too, mostly that he planned to rule Northumbria and Mercia together as a separate kingdom – which would mean the end of the Kingdom of England.

Earl Harold returned to Thorney at last, appearing out of the autumn mist early one morning when Magnus and his men were on guard duty at the bridge. The earl trotted up to the gate at the head of his housecarls, a procession of men in helmets and chainmail and carrying shields. Magnus stepped forward, but his father didn't stop. "I have to speak to the king, Magnus," he said as he rode past. "We will talk later."

But the king kept his father occupied for the rest

of that day, and well into the evening. Magnus watched the great men coming and going in the hall and felt the tension in the air. Eventually his father emerged from the king's private chamber with Stigand, and the two men stood talking quietly in the candlelit glow of the passage. Then his father strode off, nodding to Magnus to follow.

"Is Tostig dead, Father?" said Magnus. It was a moonless night, and the only light came from the torches on either side of the hall's doorway. There was a hint of winter in the cold air, and bats swooped from under the eaves, tiny black shapes that squeaked and twittered like lost souls. "Why didn't you send for the housecarls? And why—?"

"Enough!" snapped his father, rounding on him. "I have had my fill of questions for one day. Edward has whined and moaned and complained, and I'm sick of it." He paused and rubbed his face, and Magnus suddenly saw how tired he was. "I am sorry, Magnus. None of this is your fault. Your uncle lives, although it seems he has been doing his best to get himself killed."

"Sometimes we Godwins can be our own worst enemies..." Magnus murmured, and his father gave him a puzzled look. "That's what Mother says, anyway."

"Does she now? Your mother is wise as well as beautiful." The earl paused, looked at the hall, then turned once more to Magnus. "Do you trust me, Magnus?"

"Of course," said Magnus. It seemed a strange thing for his father to ask.

"I am glad to hear it," said his father, and for a moment their eyes stayed locked together. "This is perhaps the most dangerous time of all for us Godwins. Now I must get some sleep, and so must you. Tomorrow we ride to meet Tostig."

Then the earl walked away, into the darkness.

Three days later a column of five hundred housecarls with Earl Harold at its head rode into Oxford, a town higher up the Thames, north-west of London, on the border between Wessex and Mercia. Magnus and his troop were in the position of honour just behind his father. The rest of the column stretched back along the road, the men riding in pairs, the sound of hoofbeats and the clinking of harness and weapon echoing off the houses. Thick, grey clouds filled the sky and threatened rain.

"I wish I knew what the plan is once Tostig is with us," Magnus said to Hakon, who rode beside him. "Will we go to York or fight Edwin in Mercia?"

"What does it matter?" said Hakon. "We are housecarls. We do as we are bid."

Hakon was right, of course, and Magnus had already told himself he couldn't expect his father always to explain everything. But a small voice in the back of his mind disagreed. If his father wanted him to be his heir, then surely he would keep him informed. How else was he supposed to learn the arts of warcraft and leadership? Magnus sighed. It was deeply frustrating...

They came at last to a fort backing onto the river. More of the earl's housecarls were watching them from the tall wooden palisade, and Magnus heard one calling for the gate to be opened. Inside the fort was a courtyard, a large hall beyond it. The earl reined in his horse and jumped down. "Magnus, you and your troop will come with me," he said. Then he pushed open the hall's doors and strode in, most of the housecarls staying on their horses and taking up positions around it. Magnus dismounted and hurried after him, Hakon and the troop doing the same.

A dozen men were sitting on benches at the far end of the hall, their cloaks filthy and ragged, their chainmail rusty, their hollow eyes fixed on Earl Harold as he walked the length of the hall towards the lone figure standing by the hearth. Tostig was holding his hands out to the fire's warmth, its flickering red glow lighting his face. He was wearing a big bearskin cloak over his chainmail, and seemed lost in deep thought. Then Magnus realized Tostig was simply ignoring his brother.

Earl Harold stopped on the other side of the hearth from Tostig, who looked up at last. Magnus hung back, Hakon by his side, the rest of the troop fanning out behind them.

"Well, I suppose I should say better late than never, brother," Tostig muttered. "But I'd like to know what you've been up to while I've been running and hiding with the few men left to me, trying to keep Edwin from taking my head."

"I came as soon as I could, Tostig," said the earl. "I'm a very busy man. Although that's mostly because of the terrible mess you've made of everything."

"The mess *I've* made?" said Tostig. Magnus could hear the bitterness in his voice. Tostig took a deep breath, visibly getting himself under control. "Anyway, you're here now," he said, "and only one thing matters – avenging ourselves on those Mercian devils. They'll rue the day they decided to take on the Godwin family, won't they, Magnus?"

Tostig grinned at him, and Magnus smiled back, but he could feel that something was wrong. His father was behaving strangely. He had his hand on his sword hilt and was staring at Tostig with narrowed eyes, almost as if he hated his brother.

"That's not going to happen, Tostig," the earl said quietly. "You're finished."

Magnus drew in his breath sharply.

"Who are you to tell me that I'm finished, Harold?" muttered Tostig, gripping his own sword hilt now, his face dark with anger. "I am your equal, one of King Edward's earls."

"Not any more," said Earl Harold. "You've proved that you're not fit to be an earl, and Edward has decided that Northumbria should be ruled by another man."

Magnus was stunned, hardly able to believe what he was hearing. He looked to Hakon, but the house-carl had turned to the rest of the troop and raised a clenched fist, a silent signal to the troop that said, *Get ready, there might be some fighting.*

"I don't believe you," Tostig spluttered. "Edward would not do that to me."

"But he has, Tostig," said a voice behind Magnus. "You lost, and we won."

Magnus looked round. A stocky, red-haired man in chainmail had entered the hall, another man just like him at his side. A dozen warriors came in too, their shields bearing the image of a double-headed eagle. Suddenly Magnus remembered two riders on a hill, and he knew who they were before Tostig said their names.

"Edwin and Morcar…" Tostig hissed. "I'll cut out your hearts and eat them!"

He drew his sword and charged, barging between Magnus and Hakon, heading for Edwin and Morcar. Their men quickly formed a shield-wall in front of them, and Tostig crashed into it, his blade flashing in the firelight. He hacked one warrior down, the man's blood spurting across Edwin's face, but the others pushed him back.

Hakon and the housecarls had drawn their swords as well, but Tostig's men held up their hands to show they were no threat. Tostig attacked again, beating at the shields before him with his sword, screaming curses. Magnus gripped the hilt of his own sword, hardly aware of having drawn it, not knowing what to do or think.

"Enough, Tostig, lay down your sword!" Earl Harold roared, and the hall fell silent except for the sound of Tostig breathing heavily.

"What happens if I do?" said Tostig. "You'll let them kill your own brother?"

"No, I will not," said Earl Harold, his voice quieter, almost soothing. "King Edward has decided your fate will be exile. You have five days to leave England and must never return. Your wife and sons have already left, for Flanders, I believe."

Tostig stood very still. He slowly raised his sword and pointed it at his brother, blood dripping from its edge. Then he rammed it back in his scabbard and stalked out of the hall, shoving past Edwin and Morcar, his men scurrying after him.

One week later, at a great feast in King Edward's hall, two announcements were made, the first declaring Morcar to be the new Earl of Northumbria. But it was the second that froze every drop of blood in Magnus's veins.

His father was to marry Aldgyth, sister to Edwin and Morcar.

TWELVE
BROKEN HEARTS

A GREAT ROAR of approval greeted the announcement, and men banged their fists on the tables that ran in two lines down the length of the hall, or rose to their feet to offer toasts, clashing their drinking horns. The earl was sitting at the top table with King Edward on one side, and Edwin and Morcar and Aldgyth on the other. Harold took her hand and they rose to their feet to acknowledge the acclaim, both smiling.

Magnus was with Hakon at a table halfway down the hall. He rose to his feet too, his jaws clenched so hard his teeth ached, his mouth like a knife wound slashed across his face, his eyes fixed on his father. He started to walk towards the top table, but Hakon saw where he was going and grabbed his arm to hold him back. "Sit down, Magnus," the housecarl hissed. "Don't do anything stupid."

"Leave me alone," said Magnus, pulling his arm free. He kept going, right up the middle of the hall, between the tables, past cheering nobles and priests. Several slapped him on the back as he went past, shouting congratulations on his father's match, telling him he must be so proud to have such a great man for his father. Magnus said nothing, letting it all wash over him as he walked on.

The smile faded from the earl's face when he saw Magnus approaching. Magnus stopped in front of the top table, a few feet from his father, and looked at Aldgyth. She was younger than his mother, with black hair and pale skin and dark eyes, and she smiled as if she knew who he was. Her brothers were leaning together, laughing about something. Magnus ignored all three and turned back to his father.

"What are you doing?" Magnus said, eyes locked on his father's. "First you betray your brother to his enemies, and now … *this*." He waved a hand in Aldgyth's direction. "You can't marry her. You're already married. To my *mother*."

He screamed the last word and the noise in the hall died away, replaced by a buzz of people whispering, asking each other what was going on. Aldgyth's smile disintegrated. Magnus felt a presence beside him, Hakon standing at his shoulder.

"Go back to your bench, Magnus," the earl said calmly, his face stony. "This is neither the time nor the place for a father and son to speak of such things."

"Well, it seems like the right time to me, Father," said Magnus, his voice shaking. "I want to hear you explain how you can just put aside my mother so easily."

"Your father can do as he pleases," said Edwin,

staring at Magnus with cold eyes. "Everyone knows it was only a handfasting with your mother."

"What are you talking about?" said Magnus. "I don't know what that means."

"It means your parents' union was not blessed by the Church," said someone further along the top table. Magnus saw it was Stigand, and that Ealdred was sitting beside him. "So it can be dissolved when either the man or the woman decides."

"And *our* wedding will be in the king's new church," said Aldgyth, glaring at Magnus now. "Archbishop Stigand himself will perform the ceremony."

"Any other questions, boy?" said Morcar, leaning back in his seat, his rich tunic straining over his paunch. "Or can we get on with the feast? I'm starving."

Magnus looked along the line of faces, all of them staring at him, although the king seemed confused by what was going on. Magnus wished he had his sword so he could cut off their heads, but weapons were banned at feasts in the king's hall.

"Take him away, Hakon," said the earl. "We will speak later, Magnus."

"Come, Magnus," said Hakon. "We should go and sit down."

Magnus turned on his heel and walked back through the hall, all eyes following him. But he didn't stop at the table where he and Hakon had been sitting. He kept on going and strode out of the hall, with Hakon hurrying to catch up.

At dawn the next morning Magnus left Thorney alone, heading for home.

He spoke to no one for three days after he arrived, especially not his mother. Most of the time he spent hunting in the woods, although even when the hounds managed to track down a deer he didn't have the heart to make the kill. But it was better to be doing something. Otherwise he might have to listen to the voice in his head that kept telling him he had been a fool, and that he should never trust his father again.

His mother sought him out on the morning of the fourth day. He was sitting under his usual tree in the orchard when he saw her climbing the slope towards

132

him. It was cold, the sky a mass of dark clouds, the distant sea a flat sheet of grey, a soft wind whispering through the brown and yellow leaves around him. He thought briefly of trying to flee, but realized he had to talk to her eventually, and waited.

"I thought I would find you here," she said with a smile, pulling her cloak closer around her shoulders, the breeze blowing a skein of her golden hair across her face. "I know this is the place you go to when something is preying on your mind."

Magnus looked up at her. "Did you know this wedding was going to happen?" he said, his voice sounding strange to him after his long silence. "Did he tell you?"

"I only found out a little while before you did." She sat down beside him, her legs gracefully tucked beneath her. "But I always knew it would happen one day."

"Well, I wish you'd told me that a long time ago," said Magnus, ripping up grass from the ground in front of him. "I'm still not sure I even understand it."

"I'm sorry, Magnus, but I suppose it was something I didn't want to talk about." She looked down at the hall. "You know, even now I'm amazed I live in such a place... My family wasn't poor, but we weren't rich either, and families like the Godwins only marry their children to the children of other rich and powerful families. Properly marry, that is. A handfasting was the best I could ever hope for."

"But you've been together so long, and you gave birth to us, and I thought..."

Magnus stopped, unable to continue. "Don't be too hard on your father, Magnus," his mother said softly. "He's marrying Aldgyth because that's part of the price he has to pay for Edwin's support in his bid for the throne. Edwin wanted Tostig's earldom for his brother, and Aldgyth to be queen if Harold succeeds Edward. In exchange he pledged his loyalty to your father, and promised to hold the North for him."

Suddenly Magnus could see that Edwin was doing for his family what Grandfather Godwin had done for his, and what his father was doing too. He was taking positions of power, building alliances, looking to the future. But it was strange to hear his mother talking about such things. Magnus had always thought of her as only being interested in her children, and running the farm. She clearly knew about a great deal more.

"What of my uncle Tostig, though? According to my father, the family must always come first. Yet he didn't help his own brother, did he? He betrayed him."

"It's the whole family that counts for your father, not just one member of it. And because of Tostig, the family might have lost its chance to take the throne."

They fell silent for a moment. The wind strengthened, whirling the leaves around them, breaking up the clouds and sending them scudding out over the sea. Magnus felt a hot wave of shame at the memory of what he'd said to his father about sending the housecarls to save Tostig, of how he had tried to behave like a grown man and tell his father what to do. It was no wonder the earl had kept his plans from him.

"And what about you, Mother?" he said. "Will you be all right?"

"Your father is a generous man, Magnus. You are the earl's children, this is your home, and as your mother I can live here until I die. But my heart is broken."

Magnus thought his might be broken too, although he said nothing more. His mother held her hand out to him, and they walked down the slope together.

The next day Magnus helped at the autumn slaughtering. The older and weaker beasts were killed, the steaming blood drained off to be made into sausages, the carcasses butchered and the meat salted to see the farm through the winter. The work was hard and joyless, the animals squealing in terror, but Magnus knew it had to be done, and there was pleasure in seeing the farm's food stores filling up.

A week later Hakon arrived, riding into the courtyard as the sun was setting on a day that had been cold and wet. He jumped from his horse and walked up to Magnus, who was standing in the hall doorway.

The two of them looked at each other.

"It is good to see you, Hakon," said Magnus at last. "Are you here for a reason?"

"Why, I have come to visit you, of course!" said the housecarl with a smile. "I have some news for you as well. King Edward is finally coming to his end. He's been growing sicker for weeks and the priests say he will be dead by Christmas."

Edward lived through Christmas, and died at the start of the new year. Magnus's father was with him, and said afterwards that Edward had named him as his successor. Some said that was a lie, and a great assembly of nobles and priests – the Witan – was called to resolve these mighty matters of state. They argued for a day and a night, but at last they came to a decision, and heralds were sent out all over the land.

"King Edward is dead!" they proclaimed. "Long live King Harold!"

Magnus was the son of a king, and he felt less important than ever.

THIRTEEN
A RECKONING

IT WAS A hard winter, snow falling for days on end, rivers and streams and the water in the wells freezing over. Hakon stayed for a while, and Magnus took him hunting in the silent woods, although they could flush out little game from the deep white drifts that reached halfway up the leafless trees. But soon Hakon had to go back to Thorney, and Magnus sank into gloom, passing his days dozing by the hearth in the hall.

One dark afternoon a messenger walked into the hall, a young housecarl Magnus didn't recognize. Magnus's mother was sitting by the hearth too, sewing by candlelight, working on a small tapestry of Christ as a baby with his mother Mary. Gytha and Gunhild had been sent to stay in London with their grandmother, and the hall seemed even quieter for their absence. Magnus liked it that way.

"My lord Magnus? I come with a message from the king," said the housecarl, stopping a few feet from the hearth. He had snow on the shoulders of his cloak and looked frozen. Magnus kept his eyes on the fire, the word *king* calling up an image in his mind of a sickly old man. But he remembered King Edward was dead and his father was king now, and suddenly he felt his heart start to pound in his chest.

"Speak, then," he said. "What does my father wish from me?"

"He wishes you to go to Thorney, my lord," said the messenger.

"Did he say why?" Magnus asked, and realized it was a stupid question. From the moment he had walked out of the feast in King Edward's hall he had known there would be a reckoning, that he would be summoned by his father to explain why he had spoken that way before the great men of the kingdom. It had only been a matter of time. Magnus was surprised his father had waited this long.

"All I know is that he wants you there as soon as possible, my lord."

Magnus thanked the messenger, and dismissed him.

"Don't look so worried, Magnus," his mother said with a smile. "Everything will be fine."

Magnus wasn't so sure. Yet he knew there was no getting out of it.

He left the next morning, riding alone, a weak sun shining in a cold grey sky. The roads were difficult because of the snow, so the journey took longer than usual, and he spent the nights in taverns, or other farms owned by his father. He arrived on the sixth day, and the guards at the bridge gate waved him through.

His father was in the Audience Chamber, sitting on his throne. He was wearing a rich red gown of the finest cloth and a circle of gold round his brow. There were others in the room – a couple of house-carls, several nobles and priests. His father was talking to Stigand, and looked up as Magnus entered. Their eyes met, but his father didn't smile, and he carried on talking. Magnus stood in the shadows, waiting.

"Leave me now," his father said at last. "I wish to speak with my son."

The room quickly emptied, several of the men casting Magnus pitying looks as they left. He felt sick, his stomach churning, and he wondered what awful punishment his father had in store for him. When everyone was gone, his father beckoned to Magnus to come and stand before him. Then the new king leaned back and stared at him, an elbow on one arm of the chair, hand on his chin, a finger tapping his lips.

"So, Magnus," he said after a while. "We did not part on friendly terms last year. Is there anything else you want to say to me? Or do you still feel the same?"

"I'm sorry, Father," said Magnus. "I think I understand now why you had to do the things you did. I ... I just wish you had explained it all to me a little earlier."

"And what difference would that have made?" said his father. "You would still have been angry..." He paused, took a deep breath, let it out slowly. "But then I ought to have foreseen that, and what's done is done. So I forgive you, as Stigand tells me I should. Apparently forgiveness is the mark of a truly Christian king. And what about you, Magnus? Do you forgive me for what I did to Tostig – and to your mother?"

Magnus met his gaze. "I forgive you for what you did to Tostig."

His father frowned, and for a moment it seemed that he might lose his temper. Magnus couldn't change the way he felt, though. He had to be honest, whatever the consequences. As far as he was concerned, his father had done his mother wrong, even if he thought it had been for a good reason. But his father just shook his head and looked resigned. "I suppose that's the best I can hope for," he said. Suddenly he leaned forward. "Do you still want to be my heir, Magnus?"

Magnus was taken aback. "I didn't think you'd want me to be your heir, not after what I said," he spluttered. It was the last question he was expecting to be asked. He had long since convinced himself the great future he had glimpsed had vanished like the snow melting in the fields, and that his father would choose another heir.

"I didn't, at least not to begin with," said his father. "Then I realized it took courage to stand up to me like that, and I thought perhaps I should give you another chance. But I need to know I can rely on you, that you won't let me down again."

"Of course you can, Father! Is there some way I can prove it to you?"

"Well, there might be something you could do…" His father stroked his moustache with a finger and thumb. "It would be difficult and dangerous, though."

"That doesn't worry me, Father. Tell me what it is and I'll do it."

"Very well," said his father. "You can spy on Tostig for me."

Magnus felt his face stiffen, his eager expression freezing. He couldn't help thinking his father had set a trap for him and had just sprung it. "I've done that once already," he muttered, "and you didn't think much of what I discovered."

"You're mistaken, Magnus. I thought you did an excellent job of working out what Tostig was doing wrong. You just didn't like the way I dealt with him."

"But Edward sent him into exile. How can he still be a problem?"

His father gave a mirthless laugh. "I should have known my brother would make himself a nuisance wherever he is. It seems he managed to get most of his treasure out of York before he had to flee. The story goes that he had it hidden on some longships he always kept tied up in the river. He's used it to

hire more bought men and ships, and now he's raiding the coast. *Our* coast, the coast of England."

Magnus remembered the longships he had seen
when he had ridden across the bridge in York. So
his uncle wasn't quite as simple and straightforward
as he seemed. "Why is he raiding us?" Magnus said.
"What does he want?"

"Revenge, of course. But he can't invade and
defeat me because he doesn't have enough money for
an army. He raids instead, stealing whatever he can,
burning villages, killing farmers and fishermen and
their families. Perhaps he hopes the people will think
I'm weak and rise against me. Or maybe it's part of
some plan, an alliance with another claimant to the
throne. That's what I need to know."

A silence fell between them. Magnus thought
about Tostig, turning it all over in his mind. "But
how would I do it?" he said at last. "What would I
say to him?"

"You could take a ship and some housecarls who
are loyal and know how to keep their mouths shut.
Hakon will choose them for you. Then you just tell

Tostig you're on his side, keep your ears open and report back to me when you can."

"But why would Tostig trust me? In York I let him know I didn't agree with what he was doing in the North. And I am your son. I was there in Oxford when you told him he was being sent into exile. He saw me there with you."

"That's the beauty of it, Magnus," said his father. "He *did* see you there – which means he saw how shocked you were. We can be sure he also heard all about what happened at the feast. As far as he knows, you hate me for what I did to him and to your mother. So he will trust you, whatever you said in York."

"But can I trust *you*, Father?" said Magnus, the words forming in his mind and flying out of his mouth before he could stop them. He was sure his father would be angry this time – but the king leaned back in his throne and smiled once more.

"That's up to you, Magnus," he said. "I cannot decide that for you."

Magnus thought for a moment. His father had clearly plotted everything out. But then perhaps that's what kings had to do... And it occurred to Magnus that he should be taking care of his own future. Magnus loved the idea of being his father's heir, and he couldn't help feeling this was all like wading across a river – he had come too far to turn back, so he might as well carry on.

"I will do as you ask, my lord," he said at last, and knelt before the king.

Two days later a great fiery star burned across the sky over England, almost turning night into day. The priests said it was an evil omen, that it meant war and famine and death were coming, and for a while the churches were packed.

But Magnus had already set out in search of Tostig.

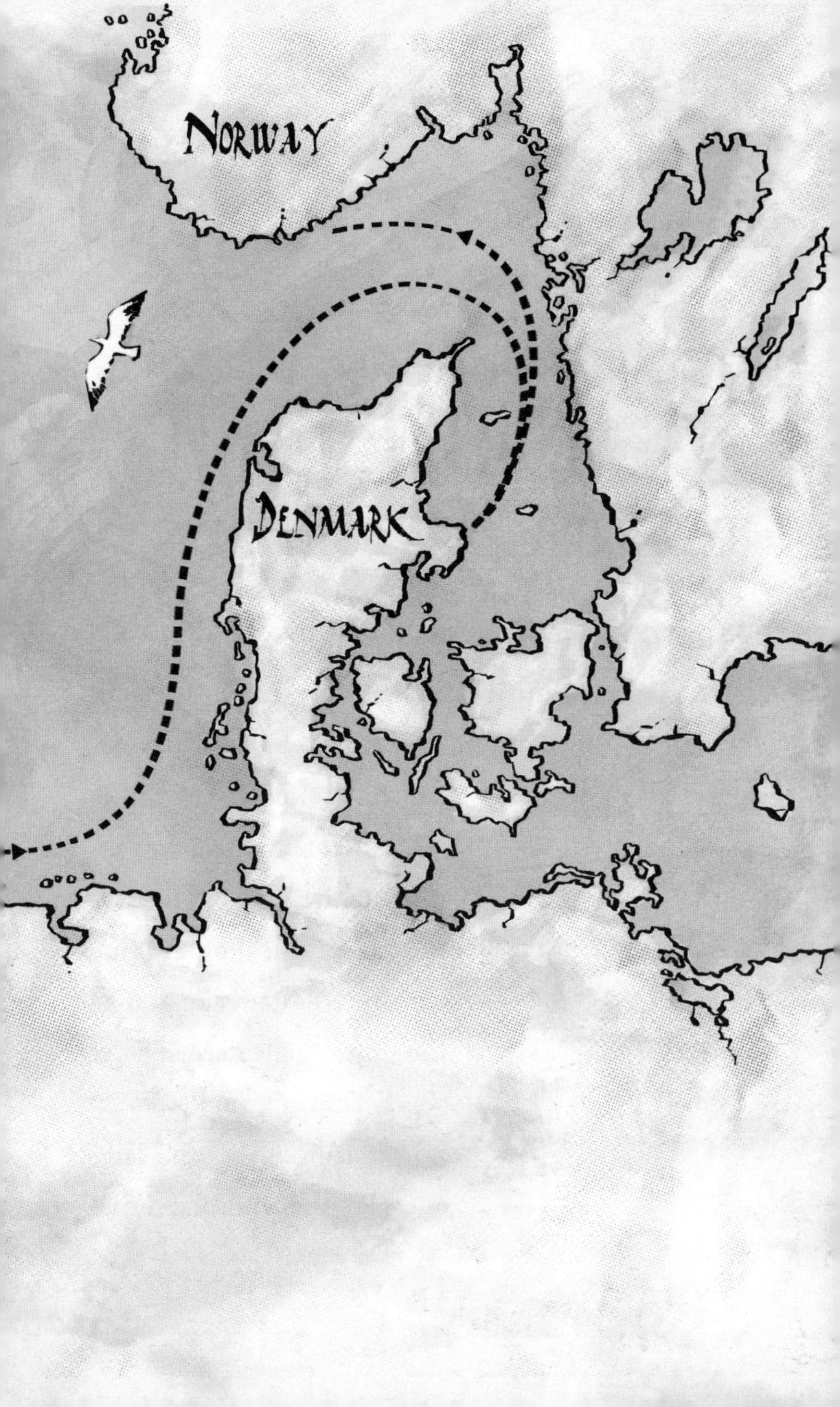
NORWAY
DENMARK

FOURTEEN

TONGUE OF A SERPENT

THEY LEFT AT dawn from a small harbour on the north shore of the Thames Estuary, in Essex, land of the East Saxons, having ridden there in secret the night before. Spring was in the air, the green water of the river sparkling in the sun, gulls squawking above the ship's single mast. There was little wind, so there was no point in raising the sail, and Hakon had ordered the

crew of thirty men to run out the oars.

Magnus stood with Hakon in the stern, the house-carl keeping the ship moving straight ahead, his touch light on the great steerboard. "You look comfortable there, Hakon," Magnus said, smiling. "I'm guessing you've sailed a ship before."

"A man may do many things in a life," said Hakon, shrugging and returning the smile. "Why, he might even spend his youth as a Viking, travelling the whale's road until he finds a generous lord to serve. And some skills a man never forgets."

"I hope one of those skills is knowing how to track down my uncle."

"That will not be hard. Tostig's raids have been moving steadily south. All we have to do is sail southwards and look out for the smoke of a burning village."

Magnus stopped smiling, remembering the column of smoke in the North, the bodies in the mud and the pools of blood.

Ahead of the ship was the open sea, and before long the wind picked up and they raised the sail. Then they flew along, the ship skimming the waves just off the low, dark line of the Kent coast. Magnus stood by the tall dragon's head prow, scanning the land.

They saw the smoke in the early afternoon. The sun had disappeared, grey clouds moving in from the east and swallowing it, but the black smudge rising above the land was unmistakeable. Hakon ran the ship onto a narrow, curved beach, shingle crunching beneath the keel. Magnus gave the order to put on chainmail and helmets, then jumped into the surf and waded ashore, Hakon and the crew following.

They climbed the rise above the beach and stopped at the top. Further round the beach they saw another ship pulled up out of the water with half a dozen armed men guarding it. There was a wide ploughed field inland, with a burning village beyond, red flames leaping, black smoke billowing. Suddenly a band of warriors came running out of the village, pursued by a larger group. Magnus saw one of the men in the smaller band turn with his sword raised – and realized it was Tostig.

Magnus groaned. "What do we do now?" he

muttered. "I can't just stand by and watch my uncle be slaughtered. But I don't think we can kill those men either."

"Why not?" said Hakon with a grin. "They all look like bought men to me, the ones chasing your uncle as well. And he might be very grateful if you save him."

Magnus glanced at Hakon, impressed yet again by the housecarl's shrewdness, and drew his sword. "Good point," he said. "Let's get on with it."

Hakon laughed, and they ran down into the field, the housecarls in their wake. Tostig's bought men saw them coming and stopped, clearly convinced they were new enemies. But Magnus and Hakon ran on past them, heading for their pursuers. They had also stopped, confusion in their faces, although that quickly changed to surprise and panic when Hakon crashed into a man and chopped him down with his axe.

The fighting didn't last long. Hakon made short work of a second man and the others began to give ground, huddling together, desperately trying to form a shield-wall. Magnus came up against a big warrior with a scarred face, and they exchanged blows, their sword blades clanging and thumping on each other's shields. Then the man broke off the fight, turning and running into the village with the rest.

Magnus set off in pursuit, his blood hot with battle-rage, but Hakon grabbed his arm and hauled him back. "Let them go, Magnus," he said. "It might be a trick. They run off into the village, you chase them – then they turn and ambush you." Magnus took a deep breath, sheathed his sword – and saw Tostig heading their way.

Tostig stopped in front of them, a lord of war in his chainmail and helmet, blood dripping from his sword, the village burning fiercely behind him. "I owe you my thanks, nephew," he said. "It seems the locals hired some bought men to protect them-selves, so you arrived in the nick of time. But tell me – what brings you to this godforsaken corner of your father's kingdom?"

Magnus shrugged. "I came looking for you, Uncle.

I thought you might need a few more good warriors to serve you. It seems I was right."

Tostig stared at him for a moment, his eyes narrowed. Then he smiled. "Well, a lord can never have too many good men. Come, it is time we made our escape." He walked off, stepping over the bodies of the dead as if they didn't exist.

Magnus glanced at Hakon, who gave a tiny nod. Then they followed him.

They sailed east then south, heading for Flanders, Magnus aboard Tostig's ship, Hakon commanding the other ship and staying close. Tostig sat with Magnus in the stern, asking him about the argument with his father. Magnus listened to himself speaking with the tongue of a serpent, the stream of lies flowing easily, and part of him felt shocked and ashamed at what he was doing. But there was excitement in it too, and a strange feeling of power – his uncle seemed to believe every word.

"I wish I had been at that feast!" said Tostig. "I can imagine the look on your father's face. And together we could have slaughtered Edwin and Morcar..."

Tostig did his own share of talking as well, complaining about what had happened in York. But he saved his harshest, bitterest words for Harold, the brother who had betrayed him. Magnus murmured and nodded, although Tostig barely noticed.

"You do know I aim to take your father's throne, don't you, Magnus?" he said at last. "Our father wanted one of his sons to be King of England – why not me?"

"Yes, I do know that." Magnus hadn't known it till then, of course, but it made sense now. "I also know my father will do everything he can to stop you."

"I have you on my side, and that means we will be unstoppable." Tostig paused, his face serious. "But are you truly on my side? Whatever might happen?"

Magnus knew what Tostig was asking. Rivalries of this kind were usually decided on the field of battle, and there would be no mercy for the loser. Magnus wondered what it would be like to see his father being killed, and felt his skin crawl as his mind filled with blood-soaked, nightmare images.

He looked Tostig straight in the eyes. "I am, Uncle," he said.

Tostig nodded. "Now all we need is an army," he murmured.

"And where will you get one?" Magnus was suddenly alert.

"Oh, don't worry, Magnus, I have a plan. I'm going to pay Duke William of Normandy a visit, and ask if I can borrow his army for a while…"

The next morning they landed on the coast of Flanders and travelled to the court of Count Baldwin, father of Tostig's wife Judith. Baldwin was old and grumpy and moaned endlessly about the cost of looking after his daughter and grandsons. Three days later the two ships were back at sea, heading west to Normandy. After a night and a day they turned into the River Orne, sailing up it to the city of Caen.

A huge new castle sat on a hill in the centre of the city, its squat towers like the folded limbs of some colossal beast ready to pounce on the tiny houses below. Tostig said they were expected, and set off for the castle with Magnus and Hakon and a couple of his men, leaving the ships tied up at the wharf.

Up close the castle seemed even more brutal to Magnus, its massive stone walls thicker than anything he had seen, even in old Roman buildings. Hard-faced soldiers in chainmail lined the battlements, and there were more inside, some practising with bows, others training with swords and the kite-shaped Norman shields. Hakon nodded his approval. "Good warriors, the Normans," he said.

Duke William was waiting in the castle's great keep. It turned out he was as squat and powerful-looking as his castle, with broad shoulders and small dark eyes that seemed to glitter with distrust and calculation, his head shaved high on the sides and back in the Norman fashion. There were others in the room, half a dozen guards in chainmail and several priests, but William was the one who commanded attention.

"Duke William welcomes you, Tostig Godwinson," said a priest in English with a French accent. The duke whispered something to him. "The

duke welcomes you also, Magnus Haroldsson, and asks when your father will keep his promise."

"What promise?" said Magnus, a chill creeping up his spine. He should have realized that he would be recognized at Duke William's court as his father's son.

"Why, to make sure Duke William succeeds King Edward," said the priest.

More than one of the Godwins spoke with a serpent's tongue, it seemed.

FIFTEEN
A FROSTY WELCOME

IT WAS A tricky moment. Tostig looked surprised and angry in equal measure, and Hakon reached for his sword. The Norman guards grabbed their sword hilts too, quickly stepping forward to form a wall of chain-mailed bodies in front of the duke. But the duke pushed through them and said something in French. Magnus guessed the duke had asked his question again.

"I know of no such promise, my lord," said Magnus, shaking his head.

The duke stared at him with those small, dark, glittering eyes, and Magnus thought it was as if they were burning off his outer flesh to see what lay inside his mind and heart. Eventually the duke seemed satisfied. He nodded and spoke rapidly in French once more, and this time the priest who had translated before turned his words into English. "The duke says you seem honest – he believes you."

"Come, we eat," said the duke, in Danish now, but with a heavy French accent. He walked off, gripping Magnus by the arm and pulling him along. "Eat – and talk."

Magnus looked over his shoulder and saw that the guards had drawn their swords and surrounded Hakon. The housecarl smiled, letting go of his sword hilt and raising his hands to show he would be no danger, then followed the duke and Magnus. Tostig elbowed his way past the guards and priests and hurried after them as well, clearly determined not to be forgotten, his face a mask of fury and frustration.

They were led through the castle to a great hall, and given seats at a long table that was set for a feast, Magnus and Tostig on either side of the duke, Hakon and the others further down. The priest who spoke English hovered behind the duke while they ate, translating as the duke shot questions at Magnus. The duke was well informed, also asking about the argument between Magnus and his father.

"I'd like to know more about this promise you spoke of," Tostig said at last.

The duke stopped eating, turned to look at him, then spoke rapidly in French again. The priest translated. "It was more of an oath than a promise…"

Magnus listened to the strange tale. According to the duke, Magnus's father had set out from Bosham on a sea voyage to London a few years ago, but there was a storm and he was shipwrecked on the Normandy coast. The duke had given him shelter, and in gratitude Magnus's father had agreed to support the duke's claim to the throne – King Edward's mother Emma had been the duke's aunt, so he and the king were cousins. The duke said Harold had sworn his oath on holy relics.

"I can believe it," Tostig said bitterly. "That sounds like my brother. He's an oath-breaker, a man who will break any promise so he can get what he wants."

"Maybe you made him swear the oath," said Magnus, looking at the duke. "Maybe you threatened to keep him a prisoner till he did. Or kill him if he didn't."

The priest translated for the duke, who scowled fiercely and spoke in French, wagging his finger at Magnus. "He did it of his own free will," said the priest.

Magnus felt Tostig's eyes on him, and realized he might have sprung to his father's defence a little too quickly. Whatever the truth of it, he remembered his task here was to find out what Tostig had in mind. "Well then, it seems that you are right, Uncle," he said, smiling at Tostig. "My father has had a busy time of it with his lies."

"He has indeed," murmured Tostig. "My brother

betrayed me, William, so we both have good cause to hate him. We should work together."

The duke's face gave nothing away, but he rose from the table and beckoned to Tostig to come with him. Magnus rose to his feet too, but the duke shook his head.

"I understand," said Magnus. "Only Tostig."

The duke nodded, and he and Tostig left the chamber, the priest scurrying after them. Magnus glanced at Hakon, who shrugged. "You will just have to be patient, Magnus," he said quietly. "Such things are not decided in a heartbeat."

In fact it was two days before Magnus heard anything. There was plenty to eat and drink – the duke had given orders that Tostig's men were to be looked after – but there was nothing to do. Hakon spent most of his time watching the duke's men practising their skills, but Magnus nearly went mad with frustration. Tostig emerged on the third day, striding angrily out of the duke's chamber.

"Come, Magnus," he said. "It is time we left this Norman dung-heap."

Within the hour both ships were heading back down the River Orne, the oars beating rhythmically. When they reached the sea they turned east, but they sailed past Flanders without stopping, and headed north along the Frisian coast instead.

It seemed that Tostig had decided to visit Sweyn, King of Denmark.

"So Duke William didn't want to lend you his army," said Magnus.

The sky and sea were grey, the land a distant dark line to the right of the ship, the sail snapping in the wind. Tostig was sitting under an awning in the stern, huddled into a thick cloak, sheltering from the icy rain and salt spray. He had been sulking ever since they had left Normandy, refusing to reveal what had happened in the duke's castle. But now he looked up at Magnus and slowly shook his head.

"I offered him a fortune if he would help me take the throne, the kingdom's taxes for a year," he said. "I even offered him Harold's earldom. But he just kept saying he wanted the throne for himself, and that he'll invade England when he's ready."

"Did he say when that might be? His soldiers looked ready enough."

"They are for the kind of campaigns he fights against his neighbours, but an invasion by sea is a different matter. It could take him months to prepare."

Magnus looked past the man at the steerboard and out over the waves. Hakon had said much the same – which meant there was no need to leave his uncle just yet.

"Do you think you can persuade Sweyn to help you?" said Magnus.

"He is a Dane, is he not? And Danes love gold above all else. I should know – I'm half Danish, and I would snap up an offer like the one I made to William."

He smiled, and by the time they reached King Sweyn's great hall at the head of Roskilde Fjord a week later, Tostig was his old self again – confident, sure he would get what he wanted. But Sweyn gave him a frosty welcome and hard words.

"I know why you are here, Tostig," he said, sitting

in a chair carved from a huge chunk of oak tree. He was a big man but no longer young, with white streaks in his long red hair and thick beard, and the belly of a man who liked to feast. His warriors stood round the hall, watching silently, hands on their sword hilts. "And all I will say is this – a man who stands between quarrelling brothers is a fool."

Tostig blustered and tried to charm him, but Sweyn would have none of it. He let them stay the night, but they left early the next morning, a couple of Sweyn's ships following them along the fjord until they were back in the open sea.

"Where now, Uncle?" said Magnus as the ship's prow hit the first waves.

"We head north," Tostig said grimly. "To Hardrada, my one last hope."

Harald Hardrada was the tallest man Magnus had ever seen, but then he was a legend, King of Norway and the greatest Viking of all time. He was more than fifty winters old, yet his back was straight, and his golden yellow hair hung down it like the mane of some legendary stallion. He gave them a much warmer welcome and laid on a rich feast in his enormous hall.

There were many longships tied up at the wharves lining the fjord below the hall, and Hardrada clearly had many warriors. The long tables in the hall were crowded with men, laughing and singing while women served them meat and ale and mead, torches burning on the walls and casting strange shadows. Magnus sat at the top table, watching and listening as his uncle talked to Hardrada.

"I hear you have been having trouble with your brother, Tostig," Hardrada said, speaking Danish with a strong Norwegian accent, his voice a deep rumble. "Why don't you settle things the Viking way? A fight to the death, winner takes all."

"I think he would accept the challenge," said Tostig, smiling. "But then he would turn up with an army at his back, and we would not be evenly matched."

"So you would need an army yourself," said Hardrada. "Yes, I can see that…"

Magnus saw a glitter of interest in Hardrada's

eyes. They talked through the feast and the next day Tostig told Magnus that he and Hardrada had struck a deal. But it had been a hard bargain.

"Hardrada promises to restore me to my earldom if I help him take the throne," said Tostig, trying to smile and failing. "It's the best I could hope for, Magnus, and at least I'll get my revenge on my brother."

Magnus felt a brief pang of pity for his uncle, but one thought filled his mind. It was time to go home – but how could he get away without Tostig knowing?

SIXTEEN
CUNNING OLD WOLF

IT TURNED OUT to be
easier than he had thought.
The next day Hardrada
decided to take Tostig hunting in the mountains. "We
need some sport after so
much talking!" he said,
slapping Tostig on the back.
Magnus and Hakon stood
at the doorway of the hall,

watching them ride off, Hardrada on a magnificent white stallion, Tostig beside him on a shaggy pony, a dozen of Hardrada's bodyguard following.

"Round up the men, Hakon," said Magnus. "We leave on the next tide."

"So soon?" said Hakon. "Tostig will guess that he has been deceived."

Magnus shrugged. At least Hakon hadn't used the word *betrayed*. "It's too late to worry about that. I need to tell my father what I know as quickly as possible."

They left later that morning on an ebb tide, Hakon steering them out to sea, the oars beating the cold grey waves, several of Hardrada's men watching and pointing from the wharves. One of them turned and ran back towards Hardrada's hall. "I have a feeling Hardrada might send a ship or two after us," said Hakon, frowning as he gripped the steerboard. "We'd better make sure we won't be easy to follow."

That meant striking out across the open sea instead of following the coast, as most voyagers did.

Such a route would be quicker, but more dangerous, although Magnus was confident enough in
Hakon's ability as a seafarer to get them safely back
to England. The journey took five days – four days
of sunshine and calm, and one of wild weather, the
ship battered by a gale. It was early evening as they
rowed at last up the Thames, the sun setting like a
ball of blood and fire beyond Thorney Island.

Magnus and Hakon jumped off the ship as soon as
its side touched the wharf, and went to find the king.
Things had changed on Thorney in the time they had
been away. There were many more housecarls than
usual on the island, more than Magnus had ever seen
in one place. A dozen burly smiths were working on
weapons of war in a big new smithy, their hammers
ringing on the just-forged, red-hot blades of swords
and axes and spears.

The king was in his audience chamber, talking to
Archbishop Stigand and several other men, including Magnus's uncles Gyrth and Leofwine, all of them
grim-faced.

"It is good to see you, Magnus," said his father.

"We will speak in private."

He led Magnus to a private chamber where Magnus told him everything that he had found out over the summer. His father listened carefully, only interrupting to ask a couple of questions. Eventually Magnus fell silent.

"You did well, Magnus, even if the news you bring me is bad," he said. "I know William plans to invade – he sent an envoy to tell me that a few days ago. He is a generous lord, and says he will spare my life and the lives of my family if I give him the crown. But I thought Hardrada might be too old for such an adventure. Now, thanks to my golden-tongued brother, I will have to face two armies."

"Did you really swear that oath to Duke William?" said Magnus.

His father frowned. "I had no choice," he said. "I had fallen into his hands, and I knew I would never leave Normandy alive unless I did what he wanted. And a forced oath isn't binding, Magnus, whatever William might say. Don't forget, King Edward named me as his successor on his deathbed…"

He talked on, going over and over the reasons why his claim to the throne was better than anyone else's, and Magnus realized his father had changed too. He seemed burdened by all that was happening, taut as a stretched bowstring, angry with the enemies who were gathering around him. Something else nagged at Magnus, and he suddenly realized what it was – his father looked more like Tostig now.

"What are we going to do?" said Magnus when his father paused.

"Two things," said his father. "The first is that we prepare for war. I have called all my housecarls together, and we are raising the Fyrd. That's what I was talking to Stigand and your uncles about. The heralds have been sent to every shire."

Magnus knew about the Fyrd. It was the name given to the army of peasants the king could summon to protect his realm, ordinary men who would leave their farms to take part in one campaign, usually with only a spear and an old shield and a leather helmet. They would never be warriors like the housecarls, but they could fill out a shield-wall, and they would fight hard to protect their homes from invaders.

"And what is the other thing, Father?" said Magnus.

His father shrugged. "We wait," he said.

It was late summer when Magnus returned to England, the month of August, and that soon turned into a bright September, the days still warm, the evenings cool. He slipped back into his Thorney routine of guard duty and training, but there was more of an edge to it now, all of them aware that something big was about to happen. Then one day, halfway through the month, a messenger arrived from the North.

Magnus was with his father in the great hall when the man strode in, his boots ringing on the stone floor. The hall was as crowded as always, although these days there were usually more warriors in chain mail present than priests. All eyes turned to the messenger as he knelt before the king and bowed his head.

"My lord, I have been sent by Edwin and Morcar

with evil tidings," he said. "The King of Norway has landed on the coast of Northumbria with a great army."

A buzz of conversation immediately filled the hall, and some men swore and yelled curses, calling Hardrada all the names they could think of. Magnus looked at his father, who sat motionless on his throne, deep in thought.

"So, it begins…" Harold murmured. Then he stood up abruptly and marched out of the hall, beckoning to the messenger to follow. "Magnus, fetch your uncles," he said. "If we are to go on the war trail, we need a plan."

They gathered in the room his father had used before he had taken the crown, and Magnus soon realized why. The best maps of the kingdom were kept there, and his father ordered the scribes to lay them out on a table. Now a group of men stood around it – his father and the messenger, Magnus's uncles, his brothers Godwin and Edmund, Stigand. Magnus was by his father's side, Hakon behind them.

His father asked the messenger where Hardrada

had landed. The man pointed on the map to the coast just north of where the great River Humber met the sea.

"Are you sure it's an army?" said Gyrth. "This might be no more than a raid."

"It's an army," said the messenger. "I didn't see them land myself, it was the coast warden who sent the news – but he said there were at least seven hundred ships."

The faces round the table grew even more grim. "That's a lot of warriors," said Leofwine. "Even with only thirty to a ship that could be as many as…"

"Twenty thousand," said Magnus's father. "But not every ship would have been full of warriors. They'll need room for horses and supplies as well."

"Even so, Harold," murmured Gyrth. "We weren't expecting so many."

Magnus's father ignored him and turned to the messenger again. "Do you know where the army is now?" he asked. "Which direction did Hardrada take?"

"I left the morning after he landed. That was twelve

days ago," said the man. "All I know is that he set off inland, heading west. They could be anywhere."

"He's making for York," said Magnus, speaking as the thought formed in his mind, and everyone looked at him. "Hardrada would have landed further south if he had wanted to attack us immediately. Perhaps he thinks the Danes in the North will flock to his banner, and he can take the rest of the kingdom afterwards. Besides, Tostig wants his earldom back."

"Wise words, my son," said his father. "The question is – what should I do about it? Should I just wait till Hardrada rides up to the gates of Thorney?"

Magnus looked down at the map and thought for a moment. "That's what he wants you to do," he said. "He thinks you will stay here in case William invades."

"I agree," said his father. "Hardrada is a cunning old wolf. He'll stay in the North while we English and Normans slaughter each other down here, then he'll swoop and gobble up whoever is still standing. So we will do the opposite of what he expects. We will go to the North and give him the biggest surprise of his life."

Then he started giving orders, and within the hour Thorney Island was a whirl of activity, housecarls rushing to prepare for the long ride to the North. Horses were saddled, weapons and armour were packed on spare mounts, the column assembled. Three hours after the messenger had first arrived, they were ready to leave.

They clattered out of Thorney over the bridge, Magnus riding just behind his father, Hakon beside him. Magnus glanced back at the men following, a giant silver serpent of chain-mailed warriors riding in pairs beneath a golden autumn sun.

Then he turned round and spurred his horse forward.

SEVENTEEN
ONE LAST CHANCE

HAROLD MADE THEM ride hard, only allowing the column to halt every night for a few hours before dawn. The men took turns to sleep in the saddle, those who were awake holding the reins of those who dozed. A nearly full moon filled the night sky with its silver glow, and the days were still warm beneath the golden September sun. But soon Magnus could barely tell the difference between the moon and sun – he was exhausted, and the nights and days had taken on the quality of a nightmare.

His father had left Gyrth and Leofwine and their housecarls – along with as many men of the Fyrd from the southern shires that they could assemble – to defend the South should William invade. He gathered more men as they rode north up into Mercia, the housecarls of minor lords whose lands they passed through. By the time they crossed into Northumbria, the column was over two thousand men strong.

"That's still not enough to beat Hardrada though, is it, Father?" said Magnus. They were riding at the head of the column, wild moors on one side of them, rocky hills on the other. "His men are good warriors, and we'll be outnumbered ten to one."

"Edwin and Morcar are pledged to fight by our side too," said his father. "They have a couple of thousand housecarls between them, and they will have called out the Fyrd of the northern shires as well."

"But what if they haven't?" said Magnus. "Most of Edwin and Morcar's housecarls are not much better than bought men. Aren't you taking a big risk?"

"Fortune favours the bold, Magnus." His father grinned, his tired face suddenly lighting up, making him look young. "And the bold are always risk-takers."

Another messenger from Edwin and Morcar brought them welcome news on the journey – they had indeed called out the northern Fyrd. Then the news turned bad. A third messenger came to say that Edwin and Morcar had decided to lead their army against Hardrada and Tostig at a place called Fulford Gate, only a few miles from York. But the earls had been defeated and forced to retreat into the city.

There were no more messengers after that, and no more news.

The king's column reached York a mere nine days after leaving Thorney Island. Once more Magnus found himself in front of the city's closed gates, nervous warriors with war bows looking down at him.

The gates were soon opened, and moments later Magnus and his father arrived at the palace, where Edwin and Morcar were waiting for them in the hall. But it was Magnus's father who took the great chair that Tostig had once occupied.

He fired questions at Edwin and Morcar. How big was Hardrada's army? What had happened at Fulford Gate? How many men did they have left? Magnus was glad to hear that Hardrada's army wasn't anywhere near as big as they had feared, perhaps as few as twelve thousand men. Edwin and Morcar still had most of their housecarls, and nearly five thousand men of the northern Fyrd had survived the battle as well. Magnus added it all up in his head – it was better, but they would still be outnumbered.

After his last question, Magnus's father sat silent, staring at Edwin and Morcar. "I guessed when I arrived that you weren't expecting me," he said at last, his voice crackling with suspicion. Magnus felt the same about Edwin and Morcar, and glanced at his father, their eyes meeting. "Perhaps you were even thinking of striking a deal with Hardrada and my brother," his father went on. "A deal to stab me in the back."

"Of course not," said Edwin, his brother shaking his head. "How could you think we would betray you, Harold? We have agreed to talk to him, though."

"Have you, now?" said Magnus's father. "What were you going to say?"

"Oh, we were going to play for time," said Morcar. "Arrange a truce, exchange hostages, that sort of thing. We knew you would come eventually."

"And ride straight into a trap," muttered Hakon, loud enough for all to hear. Edwin and Morcar glared at him, and Hakon shrugged. Harold just laughed.

"A trap is a good idea," he said. "Although I'll be the one to spring it."

Magnus felt a thrill of excitement at the prospect of battle.

But there was fear in his heart too.

Magnus snatched some sleep, but he was awake before dawn with every other warrior in York.

Edwin and Morcar had agreed to meet Hardrada that very day, at a place called Stamford Bridge, halfway between the city and the Norwegian king's camp. By the time the sun was above the eastern hills, Magnus's father was leading his army down the road towards them, Magnus riding by his side. Harold's housecarls came first, then those of Edwin and Morcar, the Fyrd tramping along behind.

They sent scouts on ahead, and one soon came riding back, reining his horse in before the king. "My lord, Hardrada is already there," he said. "But he has no more than a few thousand men with him, and most of them are not fully armed."

"So it seems that Hardrada thinks he has nothing to worry about," said Magnus's father, staring at Edwin and Morcar. Both of the brothers lowered their eyes, unable to meet his gaze, and he shook his head. "Did they see you?" he asked the scout.

"No, my lord," said the scout. "Hardrada still doesn't know you are near."

"There you are, Magnus," said his father, turning in his saddle and smiling at him. "Luck is with us today. Come, it is time to chase these Vikings from our land."

An hour later they reached a rise, the road climbing to a low ridge, and Harold ordered everyone to spread out along it, his housecarls in the centre, Edwin and Morcar's men on either side, the men of the Fyrd taking the flanks. Magnus sat on his horse and looked down at a wide brown river – the Derwent – that snaked its way through flat water meadows and was crossed by a narrow wooden bridge. Hardrada's warriors were taking their ease beyond it in the warm sunshine.

"They've spotted us," said Hakon.

Some of Hardrada's men were pointing up at the ridge. The sudden appearance of thousands of armed men must have been an unpleasant shock for them. But they were experienced warriors, and they swiftly recovered from the surprise. Those with shields – Magnus guessed there were a thousand at most – hurriedly formed a battle line on a slight mound, the yellow-haired figure of Hardrada on a tall white horse behind it. And beside him on a black horse was Tostig.

Magnus suddenly recalled the conversation with Tostig about his father's fate if Tostig should defeat him. It had seemed a distant prospect then, something that might never happen. But now there was going to be a battle – and what if his father felt the same about Tostig? Magnus shook his head, unable to believe either of them would go as far as Tostig had implied. They were family, brothers who had grown up together – surely they would step back from the brink when the moment came.

Now Harold rode forward, and Magnus tensed, expecting him to give the order for the attack. But he spurred his horse on instead, calling for Magnus to follow with Hakon and his troop. "I will give my brother one last chance, Magnus – what happens now will be up to Tostig," he said, and Magnus felt a wave of relief and hope.

Magnus's father brought his horse to a halt a spear's throw from the nearest end of the bridge. Magnus took position on his right, Hakon on his left, and the troop fanned out behind them. Hardrada had seen them, and rode up to the river with Tostig and a small band of mounted warriors. They thundered over the bridge, Hardrada and Tostig reining in their horses just a few feet in front of Magnus's father, the Viking warriors forming a shallow arc mirroring that of the Saxon housecarls.

There was quiet for a moment, the only sounds the soft snickering of horses, the creaking of saddles, the chinking of harnesses and weapons. Magnus, his father, Hakon and the rest of the troop were all in chain mail and helmets. Hardrada's men were in chain mail and carried spears and shields, but Hardrada wore only a rich blue tunic, thick silver rings on his arms, a gold chain round his throat. Tostig wore no chain mail either, just a plain tunic, but he had a sword in a scabbard on his belt.

Magnus expected Tostig to say something, perhaps accuse him of treachery. But Tostig just gave him a sad smile and shrugged, and Magnus had to look away.

"I have an offer for you, Tostig," said Magnus's father at last. "Your earldom back and more land, up to a third of the whole kingdom. If you leave Hardrada."

Magnus glanced at his father. He wondered how the king would explain that to Edwin and Morcar – and his new wife. Tostig slowly turned to look at Harold.

"Too little and too late," said Tostig. "Besides, I have made a pledge to serve my lord Harald Hardrada, future King of England. And *I* am not an oath-breaker."

They had been speaking in English, but now Hardrada spoke in his Norwegian-accented Danish. "What did he say to you, Tostig? I heard him use my name."

"He offered me my earldom back," Tostig replied in Danish. "But I said no."

Hardrada turned to Magnus's father. "Have you no offer for me, Saxon?"

"You're a big man, Viking," Harold said, also in Danish. "So I will give you seven feet of good English ground to be buried in."

Then Harold roughly pulled his horse's head

round and galloped off, back to the crest of the ridge, Magnus and Hakon and the rest of the housecarls following.

Tostig had chosen. This would be a day of death.

EIGHTEEN
THE TOUCH OF FEAR

MAGNUS'S FATHER CALLED Edwin and Morcar and the other commanders together to give them

their orders. They dismounted and gathered in a knot on the ridge, Harold in the centre, Magnus and Hakon on either side of him. "If I was Hardrada I would try and hold the bridge against us," Harold

192

said. "The river here is too deep and wide to cross otherwise. That will give him time to send to his camp for reinforcements."

"So we need to beat him quickly, before they can get here," said Magnus.

"Exactly!" his father said, slapping him on the back. "You see how well I have trained my boy?" he said to his men. "He is a warrior, a Godwin from his boots to his fingertips. Hardrada doesn't stand a chance!"

Magnus's heart swelled with pride at his father's praise, although a voice in the back of his mind reminded him that Tostig was also a Godwin.

Moments later they were mounted again and the army moved steadily down the slope, the men of the Fyrd beating spear shafts or axe-heads on their shields in time with their pounding feet. They screamed war cries and curses to give themselves courage and make their enemies afraid.

"Father..." Magnus started to say, and stopped. He was riding beside his father, so close their legs were touching. He badly wanted to ask what his father planned to do should Tostig survive the battle, but somehow he couldn't find the right words.

"No need to speak, Magnus." His father shouted to be heard above the noise, and reached over to grip his hand. "We all feel the touch of fear, even those of us who have fought a hundred battles. Trust to your sword and you will come through."

His father dug his heels into his horse's flanks and galloped forward. Magnus knew then that the moment had gone, and besides, he had begun to feel the fever of battle. So he drew his sword and spurred his horse on, Hakon at his side.

The king had been right – Hardrada's plan was clearly to hold the bridge against them. A warrior stood in the middle of it, an enormous Viking taller than Hardrada. With his shaggy black hair and beard and fur cloak over his chain mail he looked like a hulking, savage bear. He carried a double-headed battle axe, its shaft as tall as he was, and he grinned at the men gathering on the bridge in front of him.

"Come on, you Saxon pigs!" he yelled. "Who wants to go to hell today?"

Five of Edwin and Morcar's men charged. The Viking waited till they were almost on him, then swung his weapon, smashing their shields with his first stroke, lopping off two heads with the next. More men followed, but the Viking didn't give an inch, the grin never leaving his face, and soon a heap of mangled corpses lay before him, their blood cascading into the water. Another group of Edwin and Morcar's men found a small boat tied up on the bank, and they rowed it under the bridge, jabbing upwards with spears, trying to reach the Viking. Then one of them fell in.

"The fools…" muttered Hakon. He jumped off his horse and pushed his way onto the bridge, his much smaller axe held lightly in his hand. The Viking stopped smiling when he saw Hakon coming, and raised his weapon for an even more powerful stroke. Hakon leaned back and the mighty axe-head whistled past him, the razor-sharp edge just missing his face. Then he threw his own axe and the blade sliced deep into the Viking's forehead. His eyes grew wide and he fell face-down onto the heap of bodies.

A cheer went up and a mass of the king's men swarmed over the bridge.

Hardrada had put out a skirmishing line of war-riors behind it, and Magnus crossed in time to see most of them being hacked down. The few survivors turned and ran, but Magnus's father gave the order to hold back and wait for everyone to get across the river so they could form a proper line. The house-carls dismounted – as did Magnus – and the horses were sent to the rear. Before long the Saxon warriors were advancing on Hardrada and his men, weapons at the ready, shields overlapping.

Magnus scanned the bristling shield-wall a hun-dred yards ahead of him. The helmeted warriors silently stared back, their spear and axe and sword blades glinting in the sun. There were archers among the king's housecarls and the men of the Fyrd, and now Magnus heard bowstrings twanging behind him, arrows thrumming overhead, thumping into shields and Viking flesh. Gaps appeared in the shield-wall, but more of Hardrada's men stepped forward and picked up the shields of fallen men.

Sixty paces to go, fifty paces, forty. At thirty paces archers behind Hardrada's shield-wall loosed their own arrows, while others threw spears. Men were falling all around Magnus, but he couldn't allow himself to think about that. He gripped his shield straps and sword hilt more tightly and just kept walking, putting one foot in front of the other. At twenty paces they broke into a run, everyone screaming, and the Viking shield-wall locked like a great armoured beast suddenly tensing.

The two forces met with a colossal clash of wood and metal, and for a moment Magnus felt as if the world had gone mad. Both sides pushed and shoved and tried to knock their opponents off their feet. Men snarled and jabbed at each other with spears, chopped and hacked with axes and swords, their faces sometimes only a hand's breadth apart over the iron rims of their shields. Blood spurted and sprayed, and Magnus trampled on the bodies of the wounded and the dead.

A young Viking with a red beard smashed his axe into Magnus's shield, trying to yank it down.

Magnus thrust his sword at the man's face and felt the blade slice through flesh before glancing off a cheek-guard. The man ducked and Magnus raised his shield once more, expecting his opponent to renew his attack. But he didn't, and Magnus almost fell forward instead. Suddenly the Vikings were pulling back, shortening their shield-wall under the enormous pressure of the assault.

"Is this not a great fight, Magnus?" said Hakon, appearing beside him with a wolfish grin, his shield and sword and chain mail splashed with the blood of those he had killed. "Hardrada's men are almost as good as us housecarls. We outnumber them three to one, yet still they fight on. See, Hardrada has even raised his great banner Land-Waster! The poets will sing of their courage till the crack of doom..."

Magnus panted, his breath coming in gasps, and looked up the slope. The Vikings were surrounded now, the ever-decreasing shield-wall protecting the men without armour or weapons. Hardrada and Tostig had dismounted, and stood on either side of a tall staff bearing a great banner, a raven on a white background. Both of them held swords, and Hardrada was laughing as if he didn't have a care in the world.

As Magnus watched, the shield-wall was overwhelmed at last, and the final slaughter began. The Saxons moved forward, cutting down everyone in their way, a ring of steel closing round a small knot of men, the best Viking warriors of all. Finally Hardrada charged forward, screaming a war cry, and killed two housecarls with great sweeps of his sword. Then he stood at the top of the mound, swinging his sword and bellowing a song of war – until he was brought down with an arrow to the throat.

Tostig fought too, holding off a dozen housecarls even though he had no shield. He wounded one man and then another, his sword flashing in the sun and clanging on the forest of blades around him. Magnus cast aside his own shield and ran up the slope, stumbling over Viking and Saxon corpses, slipping on blood-soaked grass, desperate to make his uncle ask for mercy before he was killed. Then he saw Tostig fall.

"*STOP!*" somebody yelled in a voice that boomed across the battlefield.

The housecarls froze. Magnus turned and saw his father striding towards them, sword in hand, Viking blood splattered across his face and chest. He pushed past the housecarls, and Magnus did the same. Tostig was kneeling, and now Magnus could see he was wounded, his golden hair matted with blood, more blood running from a deep gash in his sword arm and dripping off his fingers. His face was deathly pale and he was swaying slightly, but he smiled when he saw them approaching.

"Well, this is fun, isn't it?" he said. "A family gathering on a battlefield."

Magnus glanced round. The ring of Saxon warriors stood watching and listening, hundreds of men silently staring at them. Hundreds more pressed up behind, the mound heaped with mangled bodies, Hardrada's banner now trampled and bloody. Edwin and Morcar pushed their way through the ring and stood behind Magnus's father. Something above them caught Magnus's eye, and he looked up. A small, dark shape was circling in the sunlit sky; a kestrel, or perhaps a hawk.

"It didn't have to be this way, Tostig," said Magnus's father, shaking his head. "We could have been fighting together as a family, not against each other."

"But only with you ruling the roost." Tostig's smile faded and there was bitterness in his voice. "That is how it would be, isn't it Harold? You always have to be the one in charge."

The king sighed, and put his sword back in its scabbard. Then he gently placed a hand on Tostig's shoulder, and their eyes met for a moment. "Do you have anything else to say, my brother?" said Harold, his voice soft.

Tostig turned to his nephew. "I forgive you, Magnus," he said.

Magnus stared at him, unable to speak. His father nodded and bent down to hug Tostig, fiercely kissing his cheek. Tostig closed his eyes and Harold straightened. Suddenly he unsheathed the dagger on his belt with one hand and pulled Tostig's head back with the other.

Then Harold cut his brother's throat.

NINETEEN
TIME TO MOURN

IT WAS OVER before Magnus could do or say anything. His father let go of Tostig's hair and Tostig slowly fell forward. Magnus was stunned, and couldn't tear his eyes away from Tostig's corpse, half expecting him to jump to his feet and laugh. But Tostig stayed where he was, and Magnus looked up at his father.

"What did you think would happen, Magnus?" the king said. "Tostig would have done the same to me if he and Hardrada had won the battle – and to you too."

Magnus suddenly felt something dark and dreadful inside him, a fury that writhed in his guts like a wild beast that wanted to eat its way out of his flesh. He was still holding his sword, and he gripped the hilt tightly and took a step forward. But Hakon grabbed him from behind, pinning his arms to his sides and swinging him round. "Easy now, Magnus," the housecarl whispered in his ear. "Calm yourself."

Magnus struggled for a moment, but eventually he gave up and sagged. Hakon released him, and Magnus stumbled away, barging through the silent housecarls. He kept walking until he came to the riverbank. There he threw down his sword and pulled off his helmet, hurling it to one side. Then he fell to his knees and was sick, his stomach heaving and churning until there was nothing more for it to expel.

He sat for a while, and dimly heard cheering, his father's army celebrating their victory. He knew that Hakon had followed him and was standing nearby. But his mind was full of Tostig's last moments, the images repeating over and over again until it was as if nothing else existed. Then at last there was more noise, men calling out, and the ground shook beneath him as it only does when warriors march.

"Is that the rest of Hardrada's men?" Magnus muttered, rising to his feet.

"It seems so," said Hakon. He was looking east, beyond the battlefield.

The Vikings were advancing, a solid mass of chain mail and shields, and the Saxons were re-forming their shield-wall and moving forward to meet them. Magnus took a deep breath and let it out slowly, the taste of vomit and bile still filling his mouth, his throat raw. Then he picked up his sword and started running, past Hakon and towards the new battle. Hakon cursed and hurried after him.

There were more Vikings this time, and they fought bravely, but they were just as doomed as Hardrada and the others. They were outnumbered, the men of the North felt invincible, and Harold's housecarls were as coldly ruthless as ever. Magnus grabbed a shield from a corpse and joined the shield-wall, but he didn't stay in it. Instead he pushed forward, screaming a challenge for anyone to fight him.

One Viking stepped up to take the challenge, and Magnus swiftly cut him down, then he did the same to another, and another, and yet another, until the whole Viking shield-wall seemed to melt away in front of him and there was nobody left to kill. Magnus stood alone, head back, blood dripping from his sword – and he roared his rage at the sky until his voice vanished and he could roar no more.

But the darkness was still inside him.

Hakon dragged him from the battlefield, but by then it was all over. The other half of Hardrada's army was defeated, most of them dead, the survivors begging for mercy. Harold granted them their lives, on condition they went home to Norway and swore never to invade England again. They wouldn't need seven hundred ships for the return journey. Magnus heard there were barely enough Vikings left to fill thirty. But many Saxons had died too, their corpses tangled with those of their enemies.

It was too late to return to York, so Harold's army made camp for the night. The men lit fires and sat by them, speaking of shield-brothers who had died and tending each other's wounds, or laughing as they wiped blood off weapons and mail shirts and arm-rings they had looted from Viking corpses. Some, like Magnus, simply sat in silence, hoping the flames would burn the day's images out of their minds. A housecarl had been sent to find him, but Magnus had refused to go to his father's tent. He wanted nothing from his father, and he had nothing to say to him.

"You must eat," said Hakon, offering Magnus some bread and sausage from his saddlebag. "You need to keep your strength up."

They were sitting by the fire Hakon had made against the cold of the autumn evening, the red and yellow flames leaping to the stars in the dark sky above.

"I'm not hungry," said Magnus, pulling his cloak more tightly around him.

Hakon sighed, and bit into the bread himself. "I know everything seems black to you now. You saw a terrible thing happen today, but you cannot let it destroy you. Men fight each other, and they die. You know this. Life goes on."

"Not for Tostig," said Magnus, shaking his head. "And that's my fault."

"You can believe that if you like." Hakon bit off a big chunk of sausage. "Or you could be easier on yourself. Most men would say Tostig made his own fate. It was always going to end this way for him, whether you were part of it or not."

"But I *was* part of it, Hakon. I know that, and Tostig knew it as well."

Silence fell between them, and they both stared into the flames. A wolf howled somewhere nearby, calling its pack to feast on the corpses that covered the battlefield. As far as Magnus knew, his uncle had been left where he fell. "Your father had no choice, Magnus," Hakon said at last. "Such a challenge cannot go unpunished, even if that means killing your own brother. He would have been seen as weak if he had spared Tostig. Now everyone will know just how strong a king he is."

Magnus looked at him, then lay down on the cold ground and drew his cloak over his head. He slept badly, his dreams full of slashed throats and spurting blood, and he woke with a start just after dawn to a world of pale light and white mist. Moments later a man came riding down the road from York with a message for the king.

Duke William had landed with his army on the Sussex coast.

Magnus's father marched his army back to York, where another messenger was waiting for him with more news. Men came and went in the great hall, but Magnus stayed with his troop, avoiding his father. By late morning the order to return to the South had been given, which was no surprise. Two hours later Magnus's father led the column of warriors through the gatehouse and out of York.

It was a much shorter column than the one that had arrived in York two days before. Hakon told Magnus that the battle of Stamford Bridge – for such was the name the fight had been given – had cost the lives of three hundred of the king's housecarls, and another hundred or so were too wounded to ride. Edwin and Morcar had lost many men as well.

"Yet they can hardly stop smiling," said Hakon. He and Magnus were riding at the rear of the column, as far from Magnus's father as possible. "It meant they had an excuse not to give your father any men – they claim they need those they still have to defend the North. They are just waiting to see who will win the coming battle."

Magnus didn't comment. He wasn't sure he cared any more, about that or anything else, although he did feel a pang of worry for his mother and sisters in Sussex. He was so tired he could barely stay in the saddle, and every part of his body ached. His heart ached too, but after a while he managed to empty his mind, and from then on all he saw was his horse's mane and his own hands holding the reins.

His father left him alone for the first few days on the road, concentrating on driving the column on, pushing his men even harder than during the journey to the North. Then one cold night the king came looking for his son. Magnus was lying by a fire, wrapped tightly in his cloak, unable to sleep, Hakon snoring beside him. Magnus heard footsteps approaching, and he knew who it was before his father spoke.

"Stand up, Magnus," he said quietly, and Magnus did as he was told. His father stood on the other side of the fire, the dying flames only just keeping the surrounding shadows at bay. "I have given you enough time to mourn your uncle," his father went on, his face hard and stern. "But tomorrow you must take your place at my side again. Or do you no longer wish to help me in the fight for our kingdom?"

Magnus thought for a moment, his eyes fixed on his father's. "I will help you," he said at last. "But now there are two things I can never forgive you for."

His father gave a hollow laugh. "Only two? I suppose it could be worse. And stop pretending to be asleep, Hakon – I know you are listening. We ride at sunrise."

Four days later they arrived at Thorney, and Magnus's father called a council of war. Scouts reckoned William had brought an army of eight thousand men, many of them mounted warriors. He had re-fortified the old Roman castle at Pevensey to use as a base, but he had also sent out war-bands to ravage the countryside, looting and killing and burning farms – particularly those belonging to Harold Godwinson.

"William is trying to provoke you into attacking him before you're ready," said Stigand. "Your men need to rest, and the Fyrd hasn't fully assembled yet."

Magnus's father was sitting on the throne that had been Edward's, staring into space, tapping his lips with a finger. "Well, he has succeeded," he said at last.

They rode out of Thorney the next day, Magnus

beside his father, the great silver serpent of housecarls following, weapons and armour glinting in the
dawn light.

Magnus wondered how many would meet death
at the end of the road.

TWENTY
THE MADNESS OF BATTLE
SENLAC RIDGE, 13/14 OCTOBER 1066

IT TOOK THREE days to reach Sussex, but they stopped at last on a hill crest, the leaves of the trees already partly red and yellow, the distant sea glittering under the golden autumn sun. Not much more than half the southern Fyrd was waiting there, as well as some minor lords from Wessex and Kent with their own housecarls. Magnus's father held another council of war, yet he simply shrugged when he realized his army was barely equal in number to William's.

"… And the scouts say *all* his men are real warriors," said Magnus's uncle Leofwine, Gyrth beside him with Magnus's brothers and Hakon. "They're far more experienced than the Fyrd, who make up two-thirds of our army…"

"Each of my housecarls is worth three of William's men," said Magnus's father. "So that will help to even things out. I am right, Hakon, am I not?"

"No, you are wrong, my lord," said Hakon, and Harold frowned. "I would guess that each of your housecarls is worth at least five of William's men."

Magnus's father smiled and slapped Hakon on the back, and everyone laughed. But the laughter was forced, uneasy, and Magnus knew they were all worried – all except Hakon, of course. Harold ordered the army to move on, and they took the road south, making for the coast. Several columns of black smoke rose into the sky ahead, and Magnus thought again of his mother and sisters.

Late that afternoon the scouts came racing back to report that William's army was moving up to meet them. Dusk fell, but a crescent moon provided enough light to ride through the evening. Eventually Magnus's father gave the order to camp for the night at a place called Senlac Ridge, a wide slope descending beyond it towards the distant town of Hastings and the sea. The Normans had made camp at the bottom of the slope, their fires dotting the darkness like reflections of the stars above.

Magnus helped Hakon check on the troop, making sure the men had eaten and were settled for the night. Then he went in search of his father and found him standing alone at the edge of the ridge, staring down at the Norman camp.

"Father," he said, "I wanted to ask you about Mother, and whether you…"

"You need have no fear for them, Magnus. They will be in London with your grandmother by now. I sent a troop to rescue them before we left Thorney."

Magnus felt a surge of relief. "Thank you, Father. I am glad to hear it."

"And I am glad this will soon be over. I know it has been a hard road for you, but we are nearly there. Then perhaps you and I can become friends once more."

"Perhaps," said Magnus. But he wasn't sure if he believed it.

There was movement in the camp before dawn, men rising to get ready for the day. Those with strong stomachs ate and drank, while others prayed or wished their shield-brothers good luck in the coming storm of blades and arrows. The sky cleared slowly from the east, a cloudless blue vault above them, thick white mist like a colossal fleece keeping the Norman camp hidden at the bottom of the slope. But Magnus could hear movement there too; men shouting, the neighing of horses.

His father summoned his commanders for a final council of war. They met on a small rise at the crest of the ridge, where Harold had ordered his great war banners to be set up. The White Dragon of Wessex and the Fighting Man flapped in the soft breeze that had sprung up with the dawn. Both images were on green backgrounds, the dragon roaring, the fighting man brandishing a sword.

"We will make our stand here," said Harold. "There are woods on our right and left, so William's men will have to charge up the slope to get at us, and that will tire them. My housecarls will take the centre, the Fyrd and the other housecarls on either side of them. Leofwine and Gyrth, your men will hold the flanks. All we have to do is make sure our shield-wall doesn't break, and let them wear themselves out…"

Orders were given and the men formed up shoulder to shoulder along the ridge, a rock-solid shield-wall eight hundred paces in length. Behind the front rank were three more, and behind them were five groups of a hundred men each, ready to plug any gaps that might appear during the battle. Magnus's father waited until everyone was in their place, then he rode out in front of the shield-wall.

"Men of England!" he shouted, rising in his stirrups. "This is our land, but these Normans have come here to take it from us! What do we say to them?"

"Normans *OUT*!" voices yelled, and Magnus chanted it with everyone else, all of them banging spears and axes and swords on shields. "*OUT! OUT! OUT!*"

Magnus's father drew his sword and raised it to the sky, then rode to his place on the crest of the ridge. Fear and a terrible excitement raced through Magnus's veins, his mind emptying, his exhaustion vanishing. He and Hakon were together in the centre of the shield-wall holding spears, the war banners visible right behind him if he looked round. In front of him was the slope, the Normans still concealed in the mist at the bottom. But suddenly there came an answering cry.

A voice called something in French, and thousands of other voices cheered. Then a dark mass of warriors emerged from the mist and tramped up the slope, archers and men with crossbows in front, men on foot behind. The ground trembled beneath Magnus's feet and his heart started jumping like a bird trapped in a cage. He gripped his shield straps and spear shaft tightly, lowered his helmeted head until he could only just see over his iron shield rim. That lone Norman voice called out again, and instantly the air thrummed with the sound of arrows and crossbow bolts.

Yet again Magnus felt the shock of two shield-walls crashing into each other, and found himself in the madness of battle, all the pushing and chopping and hacking. But the Normans pulled back after only a few moments. There was a pause, and then their mounted warriors thundered up the slope, men in chain mail with kite-shaped shields and long-bladed lances, on powerful horses that were like warriors themselves. They crashed into the Saxon shield-wall and it buckled – but held.

It held through the morning and into the afternoon, resisting wave after wave of attacks, the sky darkening with clouds of arrows between each one. Dead Normans and horses lay heaped in front of the Saxon line, and the grass beneath Magnus's feet was slick with blood. Many Saxons died too, but each time a man fell his body was dragged back from the shield-wall and another stepped up to take his place. Soon Magnus felt so tired he could barely hold his shield. But he fought on, determined not to let his shield-brothers down, supported by the strength of Hakon beside him.

A few sights burned into his mind, and he knew he would remember them for ever. A huge house-carl, stripped to the waist and carrying an enormous battle axe, bursting out of the shield-wall to chop down a Norman horse with one blow of his weapon, hacking off the rider's head with his second stroke, then being spitted on a lance. A Norman foot soldier leaping over the shield-wall like a wolf, killing three men before being cut to pieces. Duke William himself on a rearing horse, rallying his troops.

Then at last came the turning point. Another wave of Normans crashed into the shield-wall, but almost instantly retreated, apparently in panic. Some Saxons – the men of the Fyrd between Harold's housecarls and Gyrth's on the left – seemed to believe they had broken the Normans' spirit, and rushed out to follow them down the slope. "Stay in the shield-wall, you fools," yelled Hakon. "It's a trick!"

Magnus saw immediately that he was right. The Normans suddenly stopped and turned to face the Saxons, cutting them down as they ran. More Normans came to join in, like hunting dogs who scented blood. Then they charged up the slope again, smashing into the shield-wall and destroying the left flank. Elsewhere men of the Fyrd saw what had happened and turned to flee, leaving more gaps in the defence.

There was a brief pause as the Normans gathered themselves for one last assault. Then they came on – foot soldiers, mounted men, all of them together, determined to finish it. Magnus glanced back at his father, but a sweeping sword blow from a mounted Norman clanged on his helmet and knocked him off his feet. He lay staring at the sky, a kestrel circling high above him, or perhaps it was a hawk... Then he blacked out.

Magnus woke to juddering confusion, a clamour of voices and movement, and he realized he was being carried over someone's back, blood dripping off his face. He blacked out again, and when he next came round he was lying on the ground, Hakon kneeling over him, his brothers looming behind the house-carl. "Magnus, are you all right?" Hakon was saying. Magnus gripped his arm and pulled himself to his feet.

"I … I think so," he said, although his head throbbed. "What of the battle?" He saw now that there were fifty or so housecarls with Godwin and Edmund, a mixture of Gyrth's and Leofwine's men. They were all mounted, and had three spare horses.

"The battle is lost," said Hakon. "William's men are closing in for the kill."

Magnus looked beyond him, towards the crest of the ridge. His father's war banners still fluttered, and he caught a glimpse of his father, his sword drawn, a tight circle of housecarls around him facing outwards. But the Normans were swarming up the slope, a dark, unstoppable wave of men and horses trampling over the corpses of Saxons and their shield-brothers, and soon he could see his father no more.

"We must save my father..." he said, and tried to push past Hakon.

"It is too late for that, Magnus," said Hakon, blocking his path. "You are the one we must save now. Go with your brothers. They will take you to safety."

"What about you?" said Magnus, although he knew the answer.

"I have an oath to fulfil," said Hakon, smiling. "Live long, Magnus."

Then he ran back to the fighting, the low sun striking fire from his sword, and crashed into the Normans. Blades rose and fell, and Magnus turned away.

Darkness swooped over the land as he and his brothers rode north.

TWENTY-ONE
A FINAL FAREWELL

 THEY RODE FOR three days and nights, pursued most of the way by mounted Normans. On the fourth morning they reached London, riding at last into the city across the old Roman bridge from the south bank of the Thames. News of the battle had clearly preceded them. The

bridge guards had vanished, and there was panic on the streets. Much of the population seemed to be leaving, the wealthy in carts loaded with their possessions, the poor trudging on foot, everyone heading north.

Magnus was worn out, and almost fell from his horse when they reached his grandmother's house. His brothers carried him in, pulled off his chain mail and laid him down on a bed of rushes. He slept like a dead man till the next day.

He woke late in the morning and was soon summoned to a council of war. It was held in the chamber where he and his uncles and brothers and Hakon had spoken with his grandmother earlier that year. Now it was filled with a host of people, mostly minor lords and priests, including Archbishop Stigand, all of them arguing. Magnus's grandmother was there, and his brothers and sisters. Gunhild hugged him.

"I am so glad to see you, Magnus!" she said. "If only Mother were here too."

"What do you mean?" he said, his blood turning cold. "Where is she?"

228

"We didn't want to worry you," said Edmund. "She sent the girls to London with the housecarls, but for some reason she stayed behind."

Magnus stared at him open-mouthed, but he had no time to ask questions. "Come and stand by me, Magnus," his grandmother said in Danish, her voice cutting through the noise in the room like a sword, her eyes seemingly even more icy than ever, her cheekbones sharper. Magnus did as he was told, and she gripped his arm, her bony fingers digging into his flesh. "Stigand, tell us what you know," she said.

"Things could not be worse." The archbishop spoke in English, his face grim, and everyone fell silent. Harold was dead, his army wiped out. Duke William was making his way north, brutally crushing any resistance, burning towns and villages if the inhabitants refused to submit to him. He had also sent a messenger to London giving Harold's family and supporters a week to surrender and declare him king.

Magnus only half listened, his mind full of worry for his mother. Why had she stayed in Sussex? He remembered the columns of black smoke rising into the sky and wondered if William had already captured her, if she was even still alive... Then something of what Stigand was saying got through to him. "We could raise another army," said the archbishop. "Call out more of the Fyrd, pay for bought men."

"What about Edwin and Morcar?" said somebody. "Aren't they pledged to fight?"

"It seems not," said Stigand, shrugging. "Aldgyth has returned to Mercia, and there is a rumour that her brothers have already promised to support William."

Voices cried out in anger and disbelief and panic, and curses were heaped on the names of the northern earls. Soon everybody was arguing again.

"*ENOUGH!*" roared Magnus's grandmother, silencing them. "*WE* will fight, and we will find the men. But we need someone they can follow."

"There can be only one choice," said Stigand. "And that is ... Magnus."

Suddenly Magnus felt the eyes of everyone turn to him.

"Me?" he said, stunned, his cheeks burning.

"Yes, Magnus," said his grandmother. "We know your father was training you to be his heir. It has come sooner than expected, but that is the way of things. This is the moment for you to take your rightful place as head of the family."

"And king," said Stigand. Magnus's brothers clapped him on the back, and others cheered and called out his name, a mixture of hope and desperation in their voices.

Magnus stood surrounded by the tumult, but strangely separated from it as well. Yet this was what he had wanted – to be an important Godwin, one who would always be remembered – and you couldn't be more important than a king.

So why did he feel now that it wasn't what he wanted at all?

The council went on late into the night. Messengers came and went, rumours flew, people shouted and argued even more. As the hours passed, Magnus could sense everyone waiting for him to tell them what to do, to lead them. But he could think of nothing to say, and eventually his grandmother said he should go and rest. Magnus thanked her and hurried away, telling his brothers he wanted to be alone.

He returned to the chamber where he had woken and lay down, even though he knew he wouldn't be able to sleep. His mind kept returning to his mother. There was still no news of her, and the more he thought about her, the more worried he grew. Finally he could bear it no longer. He rose from the bed, threw on a dark cloak with a hood, and crept from the room, heading for the stable block behind the house.

He rode out of the city by the western gate, making sure nobody saw his face, and kept going westwards, avoiding Thorney Island. Then, as the sun rose behind him, he turned his horse southwards, following a narrow track through the forest.

It took him four days to get to Sussex. Four days of keeping to the little-known tracks and deep woodland, and staying away from villages. He saw few people, and those he came across ran from him, an armed man on a horse. William's route to London was further to the east, and he encountered no Normans. But burned farms and tall columns of smoke rising in the distance showed where they had been.

He arrived at the farm which had been his home on an afternoon when the sky was as grey as iron and a cold wind was gusting down from the hills. But it couldn't blow away the stench of charred timber and rotting corpses. Magnus rode through the smashed gates and saw corpses in the courtyard, people he had known all his life, arrows in their backs or their throats cut. Even the dogs had been slaughtered.

He jumped off his horse in front of the wrecked hall, its walls blackened by fire, its roof gone. He looked away for a moment, and when he turned back his mother was standing between the scorched door posts. "My son," she whispered, and they held each other for a while. Then she stood back, her cheeks wet with tears. "My prayer that you should survive the battle has been answered. What of your brothers?"

"They are safe, at least for the time being," he said. She asked about his sisters, and Magnus told her they were all with Grandmother Gytha in London.

"There is no better place for them," said his mother. "Your grandmother is a Viking down to her bones, fierce as a mother wolf when her cubs are threatened."

"But why did you not go to London too when you had the chance?"

"This is my home, Magnus, or at least it was until the Normans came. They did what you see, then took me to William. I thought he would kill me, or give me to one of his men as a reward, but he found another use for me after the battle. Only I could tell your father's body from the other dead. Oh, Magnus, what they did to him…"

She cried softly and Magnus held her again. "He is beyond all earthly pain now," she said at last. "William wanted him buried quickly, although I know where his grave is, and perhaps one day I will bring him home. Yet our new master is a generous lord. He gave me my freedom in return for finding your father. So I came back, because I had nowhere else to go. But it is not safe for you here, Magnus."

"I know," he said. He had realized that he would be killed if William caught him. William was ruthless, and would dispose of anybody with a claim to the throne. "But I had to find you, to make sure you were safe – and to ask for your counsel…"

He quickly explained what had happened in London; how they had chosen him to be the next king, the leader who would carry on the fight against the Normans.

"That is what your father would have wanted," said his mother. "But I never wanted it for you, Magnus. Power is a monster that eats all those who strive for it."

She was right, of course. Magnus thought of Tostig and his struggles, of Hardrada and his wish for glory, and of his father's great plans and plots and schemes. They had all ended in blood and slaughter, in burned farms and battlefields strewn with corpses. He knew that to defeat William he would have to be just the same as them, and be prepared to do the same kind of things they had done – or even worse.

"Is it not my duty, Mother?" he said quietly. "After all, I am a Godwin."

"You are much more than that, Magnus. You are a son and a brother, and a fine warrior. And sometimes it is braver to say no than it is to do what others want. There could be another life waiting for you, in another land, with other people."

The wind had dropped, but now it returned, scuffling round their feet and tugging at their clothes and hair, the horse tossing its head and snickering. Magnus felt his heart rise, most of his doubts and fears vanishing. He knew now what he wanted to do, and realized that deep down he had always known. That was why he was here, seeking his mother's blessing to leave, rather than in London being a king.

But there was still one worry that nagged at him. "What about you?" he said to her. "If I go I can never come back. I won't be here to protect you or my sisters."

"I can take care of myself, Magnus." She laid a cool hand on his cheek and kissed him. "I will find an abbey to take me in, and live a life of prayer, and your grandmother will look after your sisters. You must think only of your own future."

Magnus hugged her one last time and climbed back onto his horse.

Then he rode away, heading west, towards the setting sun.

HISTORICAL NOTE

MAGNUS REALLY LIVED – his name is recorded in several of the original sources. Most of the other characters are real too. Hakon and Gisli are fictional, but there were certainly men like them in the eleventh century, a time of violence and war.

William of Normandy was crowned King of England by Archbishop Ealdred on Christmas Day 1066. William allowed Stigand to remain Archbishop of Canterbury until 1070, but then had him put in prison, where Stigand died a few years later. William died in 1087, and was succeeded by his son, another William.

Magnus's grandmother Gytha did gather more men and fought on, retreating at last to Exeter in Devon, where William besieged and defeated her in 1068. After that she made her way to the court of King Sweyn in Denmark, taking her granddaughter Gytha with her. The date of the older Gytha's death is not recorded.

Magnus's brothers also fought on, ending up in Ireland, from where they launched raids against William before fading from view. Edwin and Morcar tried to make friends with William, but also rebelled. Edwin was killed in 1071 and Morcar died in a Norman dungeon in 1087. William finally crushed all Saxon resistance.

Magnus's sister Gunhild became a nun, and Sweyn arranged for his other sister, the younger Gytha, to marry Prince Vladimir of Smolensk in what is now Russia. Many of her descendants married into the royal families of Europe. Our current queen is distantly descended from her – and from William of Normandy.

Magnus's mother is thought to have spent the rest of her life in an abbey.

Nobody knows what happened to Magnus. He walked out of the pages of history in the autumn of 1066.